FAMILY IN A TREE

JAMES HORSLEY

CRANTHORPE
MILLNER

Best Wishes,

James Horsley

X

First published by Cranthorpe Millner Publishers (2022)

ISBN 978-1-80378-009-2 (Paperback)

www.cranthorpemillner.com

Cranthorpe Millner Publishers

About the Author

James Michael Horsley was born on the coast of Britain's East Anglia in the last few years of the twentieth century. His parents are musicians, and they introduced him to the arts from a young age. At seven years old, he moved with his family into the countryside, where he could shape his artistic creativity more peacefully and effectively. During late adolescence, he was drawn to performing arts, but never far from writing stories. He is also an actor, a singer and a former dancer.

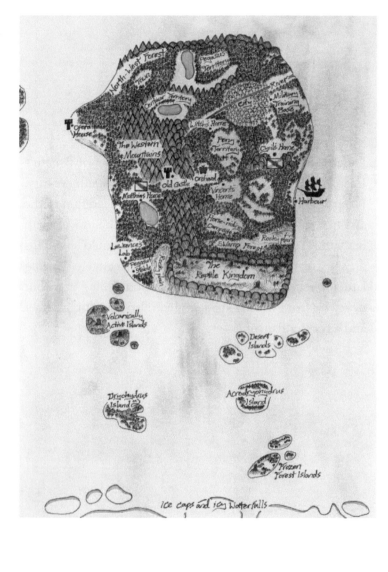

PROLOGUE

Once upon a time, there was a map on the page of a book, a book called Family in a Tree, and this map depicted a land upon which lived countless fantasy creatures. The land was ruled by a king and queen, and our story begins with the birth of their son, whom they named Cyril.

This trio of royalty lived together inside a ginormous tree, the size of a stately home, which stood atop a small grass-covered hill. A long, golden fence was built around the hill, although a wall round the back faced the forest. The tree's enormous trunk was enclosed within a square-shaped walled structure, featuring a tall tower at each corner. On the opposite side of the concrete structure to the entrance was the back garden, where there was not only a patio but also a wooden horse stable built alongside. The entire tree was small for a palace household and had passages running through the hollow roots, large enough for a human-sized being to walk down. Many of these passageways had looping branches growing inside them, where small grass snakes could often be found resting, enjoying the relative warmth of the passages. A building on the slope of the hill accommodated a small army of soldiers and guards. Halfway up the hill, standing almost as tall as the great tree itself, was the royal flagpole, its flag now featuring a medallion to represent the birth of the heir to the throne, Prince Cyril.

Cyril was a loveable and energetic baby, with bright blue eyes and wispy white hair, a treasure to both his parents and the Kingdom. But while he seemed joyful most of the time, his eyes would occasionally grow anxious, as if he were thinking deeply. His mother, the Queen, was a slender and majestic-looking woman, with graceful dark hair which she usually wore tied back into two long plaits, and a face which very much resembled her son's. She was generally more concerned and considerate than the King, especially when it came to Cyril. Cyril's father, the King was more sturdily built than his wife, and his curly blonde hair and pale complexion were responsible for Cyril's colouring. The King had a good sense of humour and would spend a long time playing with Cyril, delighting in his peals of laughter. But much as they adored spoiling him, both the King and Queen knew that their little one would have to be well-raised and well-taught if he was to rule the Kingdom one day.

The members of the royal family were all human, with bright, attractive complexions, but this was not the case for most of the people they ruled over. Indeed, their Kingdom was home to numerous different creatures of all shapes and sizes. Some had vibrant head crests; others had long, perfectly manicured claws; a few had large, almost translucent ears, and many of them had tails. As such, there was a great deal Cyril would need to learn about the Kingdom before he became its ruler.

At six months old, Cyril was baptised and was taken by his parents into the city so that the public could meet him. This meeting was to take place during a great feast in the young Prince's honour, at Hugo and Henry's Hall. It was inside a vast pavilion encompassing both a restaurant and a ballroom.

All the guests, regardless of their physique, would be very formally dressed: the men in long coats and frilly shirts and the women in elegant ball gowns and hats.

The weather was sunny when the King and Queen arrived at the Hall on the day of the feast, so they decided to take Cyril up into the garden on the roof of the Hall to enjoy a moment of quiet before the party began. There they came across Henry and Hugo, the owners of the hall, who they greeted warmly, shaking them both by the hand.

'Congratulations, Ma'am,' said Hugo. 'May I say that any new arrival is a joy to behold at this hall?'

'Thank you, Mr Hugo,' the Queen replied. 'We appreciate having the opportunity to come here. I believe your daughter was born recently also?'

'Lydia, yes.' Hugo turned to a toddler nearby, his daughter, Lydia. Like her father, Lydia had pointy ears, two small, symmetrical head crests and a tail with hairs on the end. Her crests were just visible with her hat on.

'She will be two in a few weeks,' Hugo went on. 'Her eyes are as yellow as mine already.'

Hugo continued his conversation with the Queen as Lydia turned and caught the eye of little Cyril. The two children waved to each other, but Cyril was holding a handkerchief, and promptly dropped it on the grass with a chuckle. As the King and Queen turned to walk away, Lydia toddled over to the handkerchief. She picked it up and held it up to give to Cyril, but the royal family had disappeared.

'Hanky...' mumbled Lydia.

Her mother beckoned to her. 'Lydia?'

Lydia turned round and toddled over to her mother, a ginger haired woman with pink eyes who was holding a baby of her own.

'Hanky,' repeated Lydia, holding up the handkerchief. 'Baby hanky...'

'Oh, thank you,' said her mother, taking it from her and giving it to her own baby.

'Mamma?' said Lydia. 'Prince, he...'

'Yes, love,' her mother sighed. 'One day you'll find a handsome prince and live happily ever after, when you're a big girl, of course.'

Lydia put her finger to her lips and looked in Cyril's direction, as her mother pulled her gently away.

CHAPTER I

NAUGHTY MONKEYS

One sunny day, many years later, the King and Queen were in their throne room. As usual they both wore their crowns. The Queen was in her lilac dress, gazing out of the window, while the King was wearing his scarlet robe, standing behind her.

'Wouldn't it be best if he remained here, where we know he's safe?' asked the King.

The Queen turned round.

'That's the problem. Cyril spends too much time here; he's got to get out more and see the real world.'

'What's the worst that could happen?' the King went on. 'Couldn't one of us go with him?'

5

The Queen tore her gaze away from the window and walked anxiously to her throne.

'I admit…he does still play with his stuffed toys and…apply his imagination to mere doodles and drawings,' she stuttered. 'But he's grown up now and needs to become more independent if we are not to abdicate in favour of Matthias. If I don't attempt to persuade Cyril now, I do not know when it might happen.'

She crossed the floor of the throne room and walked through the large wooden doors. The King followed as they made their way up a staircase.

'So, the plan is to talk Cyril into venturing out by himself, to make him realise how much he needs to mature?' confirmed the King.

'He does still have a great deal to learn,' said the Queen.

They continued to climb the stairs, past the paintings and greenery, and soon reached a single wooden door. The Queen knocked and waited.

'Come in,' came a voice from behind the door.

The King and Queen entered and found their grown-up son sitting on his bed, playing with his stuffed toys. He was dressed in his usual white shirt, cream waistcoat, white knickerbockers and tights. He had straight, golden hair and a low, baritone voice, but not a vast vocabulary.

'Mum, Dad, hello,' he said. 'You're just in time; my toy unicorn has been ripped. He and the dragon were fighting and…well, he has a hole and stuffing's coming out.'

'Were they really fighting, or did you just make them fight?' asked the King.

'I may have overdone it a little,' Cyril admitted.

'Don't worry,' the Queen reassured him. 'I can fix that for you.'

'I love you, Mum.' Cyril gave her a hug.

'Now, Cyril, darling,' the Queen began. 'I think you should go out today and get some fresh air.'

'Okay, when shall we go?' Cyril asked.

'We're not…we're not coming, Cyril,' said the Queen.

Cyril looked puzzled, as his mother sat down with him on the bed and continued.…

'You can take Finnegan with you, but we want you to become more independent. We want you to learn to go out into the world without me or your father accompanying you. I'm sure you've always wanted to do that.'

'Well…now that you mention it, this weather has disturbed me,' replied Cyril. 'Maybe it's the urge to go out.'

'Why don't you give it a try, then?' encouraged the Queen. 'You'll never know until you give it a go. Finnegan will keep you company.'

'Alright,' said Cyril. 'I'll go now, then.'

He stood up, but the Queen sat him down again.

'If you come across any of our friends or relations, behave yourself, yes? No lying and no unnecessary physical contact, have I made myself clear?'

Cyril had a mischievous glint in his eye.

'Okay, then,' he replied. 'But promise me you'll stay here, so that I know where you are.'

'Of course, we will…won't we?' The Queen turned to the King.

'Yes, of course,' the King agreed.

The Queen gave Cyril a kiss on the cheek, making him squirm.

'Don't kiss me, Mum, you know I don't like it!'

'Sorry,' said the Queen, placing her hand on his shoulder.

'But…it is okay if you kiss me when I'm hurt,' Cyril added.

'Very well,' said the Queen.

She allowed Cyril to stand up and take his coat from the back of his door. It was a long, scarlet coat, complete with epaulettes and the medallion on the breast.

'Where are my shoes by the way?' he asked.

'In the main downstairs passage, by the door leading to the stable,' replied the Queen.

Without another word, Cyril left the room and made his way downstairs. The Queen looked at Cyril's toys and sighed. Then she looked at the King again.

'The world is cruel sometimes, but we have to give our offspring an opportunity or two.'

'Exactly,' said the King. 'We don't want to make it any worse.'

'Now,' said the Queen, picking up Cyril's ripped unicorn toy. 'I suppose I'd better knit Humpty-Dumpty back together again.'

Meanwhile, Cyril had made his way to the stable. The royal stable currently accommodated four horses, one of which was Cyril's own horse, Finnegan, who had a clean, white coat and golden mane. He was busy eating his way through a trough full of food.

'How's the new feed?' asked Cyril.

'Well, I think I have another favourite meal,' replied Finnegan, looking up. 'It's delicious.'

Cyril gave him a pat and prepared a bridle and saddle.

'Where are we off to today then, Cyril?' asked Finnegan. 'And where are your parents?'

'They're not coming. They wanted me to go out alone.'

'Ah, yes, it took much longer than I thought,' said Finnegan. 'But the time has finally come.'

'Yes, alright,' said Cyril, somewhat irritably. 'Now, come on. Let's get you ready…if I can remember how to do this…'

He managed to attach Finnegan's bridle securely to him and put the saddle on the horse's back. Then, he opened the gate of the horse's pen and brought Finnegan to the stable doors, beyond which a lush, green landscape beckoned.

'This is going to be just fine,' Cyril said, calmly, as he walked Finnegan out of the stable and down to the bottom of the hill towards the back gate.

The King and Queen were, by this time, relaxing in their aquarium room. It was a stylish chamber, featuring a smooth, marble floor and a large pool filled with goldfish. There were also a few tanks dotted around the chamber, containing other marine animals.

The Queen was busy mending Cyril's stuffed toy, a task she had undertaken so many times that she could do it whilst gazing into a tank of sea horses and bright orange sponges.

'These are some of the oldest and most primitive forms of life, aren't they?'

'Indeed,' said the King, strolling around the room, stopping to observe a tank with three purple starfish stuck to the bottom. 'You would never believe that the ancestors of all animals came from the sea. But I suppose water is the chemical that holds all life together.'

'There, that should do it,' said the Queen, holding up Cyril's unicorn and admiring her handiwork. As she stood up, she turned back to the overfilled filing cabinet, where she kept her wool and needles. 'Oh, goodness, I had best clear out all this paper. The cabinet's stuffed.'

She walked over and began clearing it, glancing at some of the papers as she did so.

'Did you know all these old bills were here?'

'What bills?' asked the King.

'The bills we received while taking care of Cyril. There are so many.' The Queen continued shuffling the parchment until she found something that made her freeze.

The King turned around at her sudden silence. 'What is it?'

'Do you remember what date we arranged to have luncheon…at Matthias's?' asked the Queen.

'No, it must have slipped my mind,' said the King.

'Well…' the Queen went on. 'Ironically, it's today. I was thinking it had been a while since we had a meal at your brother's, that today was feeling too bright and empty. Honestly, I was sure I put it in the diary ages ago.'

'We had best hurry,' said the King. 'We could still get

there by lunchtime if we set off soon. Come on, let's get ready.'

'Wait!' exclaimed the Queen. 'It's not that simple. We promised Cyril we would remain here while he went out. We dare not go back on our word.'

She turned to face the King and took his hands. 'What are we going to do?'

'It's alright, I've got a plan,' said the King. 'If we travel to Matthias's by the fastest possible route and only have a short bite to eat, we should beat Cyril back home.'

'That's insane…' the Queen sighed. 'But we can't cancel on Matthias this late. I suppose it could work. Get Trevor and Gillian ready then. I'll fetch the cloaks.'

The King scrambled out of a nearby door and quickly headed towards the stable, while the Queen, lifting up her dress, rushed back up the indoor staircase.

'I just know I'm going to regret this.'

After a while, Cyril and Finnegan came to a beach.

'I wonder where this beach leads to?' pondered Cyril.

'To the big city, I should think,' said Finnegan, as they continued pacing down the beach.

Suddenly, a few steps behind the two friends, a strange figure emerged from the tide. The figure was a male humanoid, a creature with arms, legs and a human-like head, but from its back grew a long tail, with hairs on the tip; it's head-hair was long and matted, it had two large, pointy ears and its skin was pale grey with dark grey stripes. So as to avoid attracting Cyril's attention, the creature slithered onto the shore and gradually stood up, slowly and subtly stalking the young Prince and his steed.

'It's a bit too quiet,' murmured Cyril to Finnegan.

'Yes…wait, look, Cyril,' said Finnegan, quickly. 'There are some trees just over there and…it looks like there might be people too.'

As Cyril squinted at the trees, the humanoid creature appeared before them, causing them both to stumble backwards in surprise.

'Forgive me, O noble rider,' said the strange being. 'I mean you no harm.'

'How can we be sure?' Finnegan asked. 'Who are you? And what do you want with His Royal Highness, Prince Cyril?'

'It's okay,' said Cyril, climbing off Finnegan. 'He looks harmless. What…what can I do for you?'

The humanoid being put his arm round Cyril's shoulder and walked him further down the beach. Finnegan followed.

'I am the marine primate of the East Beach; my kind are known as Thalassopithecus.'

'Oh…?' said Cyril.

As they walked on further, towards the trees, Cyril and Finnegan failed to notice that a whole tribe of thalassopithecus, male and female, were emerging from the waves. Soon, Cyril, Finnegan and their new acquaintance arrived at the concentration of trees.

'This is where my friends and relatives dwell,' explained the primate.

'Yes, I can see that,' Cyril replied.

The trees were full of thalassopithecus, talking and

laughing with one another, with groups periodically splitting off and slithering towards the sea.

'This looks like fun, I wish I were one of you,' sighed Cyril.

'Unfortunate, is it not?' replied the primate. 'But I have one question…' he added, as his friends sneaked up alongside Finnegan. 'Why are you upside-down?'

'Upside-down?' said Cyril, puzzled. 'But…I'm not upside-down…'

His words were cut off by an exclamation of surprise, as he took a step back onto a trip wire, which instantly tightened, lifting Cyril up so that he was hanging by his ankle.

'You are now!' laughed the primate, and the rest of the tribe laughed with him.

They then started mocking Finnegan, poking his hide and playing with his bridle. They were clearly a group of troublemakers.

'Oh, dear,' said Cyril to himself, as he hung upside-down. 'I think I had best try and get us out of here.'

Folding himself in two with the strength of his stomach, Cyril slowly used his hands to work his ankle free and, at the same time, hung onto the rope to keep himself from falling. Once he was free, he dropped himself back down onto Finnegan's saddle, making the horse rear up on his hindlegs and almost start bucking in surprise. Immediately, the creatures scrambled back into the trees and into the sea, as Cyril adjusted himself in the saddle.

'What…Cyril?' stuttered Finnegan, as he settled down.

'Yes, Finnegan?'

'That was quite sudden and unexpected. What's the plan now then?'

'Let's go to the opposite beach and hope that we don't find any more of these monsters,' suggested Cyril. 'Come on, we'll go into the trees and through the forest.'

The King and Queen had arrived at the home of Cyril's uncle, Prince Matthias. He was the only other person in the Kingdom to have made his home in an enormous tree. It was just like their own tree, only with the walls and towers a darker colour, rickety bridges connecting the towers and a slightly different flag. There was a lake in the background, and the hills were green with brown streaks. The King and Queen stood outside the main gates beside their horses, Trevor and Gillian.

'This place hasn't changed much,' muttered the Queen.

After a moment, a royal guard appeared at the gates, dressed in white tights, a blue coat with epaulettes and a hat.

'Your Majesties,' he said, bowing. 'Is His Highness expecting a royal gathering?'

'Nothing quite so formal,' said the Queen.

'We just need to pay my little brother a visit,' said the King.

The Queen coughed.

'I mean, pay the Prince a visit,' corrected the King.

'By all means, Sir,' said the guard, opening the gate.

The King and Queen entered, guiding in their horses.

Cyril and Finnegan were emerging from the trees,

towards the coast on the opposite side of the landmass. They were still travelling beneath the trees and amongst beanstalks and toadstools, but the sea was now in view.

'We're nearly there, Cyril,' said Finnegan. 'Nearly at the West Beach.'

'Good,' replied Cyril.

As they drew closer, Cyril caught sight of a building in the distance. It was a lodge, with red beams, white walls and cross-hatched windows.

'What's that building over there?'

'That's the laboratory of Lawrence Toadstool,' said Finnegan. 'The scientist, remember?'

'Oh, no, not that bloke,' groaned Cyril.

'What's wrong with him?'

'He never stops talking. His lectures are impossible to keep up with…'

Just as they were about to leave the forest behind, another human-like primate dropped down from a branch in front of them. This one had green skin, curly hair, pointy ears and a tail, but it also had two mushroom-shaped crests on its head.

'Oh, not again!' cried Cyril.

'What be this being on the top of another?' asked the creature, as Cyril climbed off Finnegan.

'I'm Prince Cyril,' said Cyril. 'And…I'm not…we…we are plants.'

The creature clapped his hands, and just like before, the rest of the tribe suddenly descended from the trees.

'No!' yelled Cyril. 'This can't be happening!'

The creature moved closer.

'Be you plants for certain?' he asked.

'No, we're animals,' said Finnegan. 'The Prince has already been through enough trouble caused by the likes of you.'

'Wait,' said Cyril. 'If they are plant-eaters, maybe they really are harmless.'

'You are quite right, Your Highness,' said the creature. 'I am a beast from the South, with crests; my kind are known as Australophotherium.'

'Crests?' said Cyril.

'Referring to these here outgrowths upon our heads,' said the primate. As he spoke, his head crests turned a rich, vibrant red, as did the crests of the rest of the tribe.

'That's…disturbing,' said Cyril nervously, as he began to walk backwards.

The tribe started to walk towards him, and Cyril continued to back away, unintentionally walking onto one end of a wooden teeterboard. Up in a tree behind him, two other members of the tribe suddenly jumped down onto the other end of the teeterboard, sending Cyril flying through the air, before he landed in a pile of twigs.

The tribe laughed, and just as before, began to tease Finnegan. Finnegan spoke severely to them, but it was no use.

'I don't believe it,' Cyril said to himself, climbing out of the twig pile. 'I suppose I will have to try something a little more…dangerous.'

He picked up two twigs and rubbed them together to create a flame, and it wasn't long before the whole pile of twigs was set alight.

'Fire!' he yelled.

The tribe shrieked and scurried away in the trees as Finnegan came over to Cyril.

'What have you done, Cyril?'

'Well, Mum told me not to play with matches,' said Cyril. 'So, I played with twigs instead.'

'Fire?' came a voice from the distance.

Cyril and Finnegan turned to see a more human-like figure approaching them, with claws on his fingers and horns on his head, but no tail. He was also wearing clothes: a long brown coat, tights and a frilly shirt.

'That's Lawrence Toadstool,' Finnegan whispered to Cyril.

Cyril's worried expression was quickly replaced by a look of determination as an idea came to him, and he began to walk towards Lawrence. Meanwhile, Lawrence started running, straight past Cyril, towards the fire. Cyril followed.

'Come on,' said Lawrence, taking off his coat. 'We must extinguish this fire!'

As he started to beat the fire with his coat, Cyril took off his own coat and did the same.

Once the fire was out, Lawrence looked up at Cyril, suddenly recognising him. 'Prince Cyril?'

'Yes…that's me,' replied Cyril.

'An extraordinary surprise meeting you here, Your Highness,' said Lawrence as he shook Cyril's hand. 'What brings you here?'

Cyril thought quickly and stuttered an explanation. 'Those…things…they…kidnapped my parents and are now heading for the East Beach.'

'Oh, my goodness,' said Lawrence.

'I was just about to go after them,' Cyril went on. 'Could you…?'

'Say no more, Your Highness…' interrupted Lawrence. 'I shall help you. Just allow me to get my horse.'

He put his coat back on and ran back towards his laboratory.

'I'll go after them now!' called Cyril.

'By all means, do that!' Lawrence yelled in response as he disappeared from view.

'Why did you tell him that, Cyril?' asked Finnegan, astounded. 'It's not true.'

'I needed to get rid of him so that the conversation would end,' shrugged Cyril. 'I want to find out why two very similar types of creatures are living on both sides of the mainland. It doesn't make sense and I don't want Lawrence to stop me from finding the answer.'

They continued riding for a short while until, as they came over the crest of a hill, they found the city. It was surrounded by a great wall but with a clear gap for visitors and citizens to enter through.

The two friends moved closer and within minutes had reached the brick road within the city, passing streets full of commoners' houses, with their black beams and white walls.

'Where exactly are we going, Cyril?' asked Finnegan.

'To the house of Mel Blue-Bottom,' explained Cyril. 'He's an old author and explorer. *He'll* know the answer to my question.'

When they had ridden around a few more bends, they came to a bungalow nestled behind a small white fence. The house was long rather than tall, almost tunnel-like in appearance, and probably didn't have room for many people to walk inside at the same time. The name, 'Mel Blue-Bottom' was etched on the door.

'This is it, Finnegan. Stop here.'

Finnegan stopped and Cyril climbed down and walked over to the front door. He then rang the bell and waited.

After a moment, an elderly but good-looking man opened the door from the inside. It was Mel. He had curly, grey hair and was wearing a long, dark-red coat and glasses.

'Ah, Your Royal Highness,' he said, shaking Cyril's hand.

'Hello, Mel. I mean…Mr Blue-Bottom,' said Cyril. 'I want to talk to you about those creatures that live on the coasts. You know what I mean, the troublesome ones with tails, sometimes swimming?'

'Ah, yes,' said Mel, stepping aside. 'Of course, Your Highness. Do come in and I shall prepare you some tea.'

A few minutes later, having left Finnegan outside, Cyril and Mel were both sitting in the living room, drinking warm cups of tea. It was a very confined space, with a bookshelf on one side and a window and fireplace on the other.

'So, how did those creatures…well, end up where they are now?' asked Cyril.

'It is down to a remarkable twist in nature, Your Highness,' said Mel. 'But I will gladly explain how it occurred. You see that big brown book over there? The one with the green stripe?'

Cyril came over to the bookshelf and took the book Mel was pointing to.

'That's the one,' said Mel.

Cyril began flipping through it, captured by the contents and illustrations.

'This looks amazing,' he said. 'But it's quite complicated.'

'Allow me,' said Mel, as Cyril handed him the book.

Mel began to flip through, before finally settling on a page. 'Ah, here it is…'

Cyril listened as Mel started reading.

'*Some forty years before the first monarch, the southern tip of the mainland was smaller and narrower and was surrounded by many islands, inhabited by small mammals.* 'Mammals' refers to a diverse range of animals, from mice to elephants to human beings.'

'*Us?*' exclaimed Cyril.

'Yes, apparently,' said Mel. 'Strictly speaking, you are an animal too. Mammals produce milk and give birth to live babies, instead of laying eggs. Well, most of them do.'

He continued to read. '*One devastating evening, volcanic activity broke one of these islands in two, an island inhabited by monkeys. One half drifted towards a lagoon, on the South-West side of the mainland, while the other approached the East side. They crashed violently into their resting places, destroying cliffs and buildings on both coastlines. Scorching-hot, orange liquid was still pouring out from the volcanic eruption, and this liquid slowly ran out onto the beaches, eventually solidifying and forming a hard, rocky ground.'*

'What's this got to do with those creatures?' asked Cyril.

'Well, now,' said Mel, turning a page or two. 'The monkeys that landed on the East coast developed the ability to swim and began to feed on meat, but those that had landed on the West coast lived in the forest, feeding entirely on plants. As centuries passed, both groups kept having babies, and each generation of babies was slightly different to the one before. They became larger, more upright, until eventually, they were no-longer monkeys, but...'

'Thalassopith…and australoph…' began Cyril.

'Thalassopithecus and Australophotherium,' Mel corrected him. 'Because the original troop of monkeys was separated by the eruption, the two new groups ended up transforming into very different creatures, simply because their new lifestyles and habitats were so different.'

There was no reply.

'Your Highness?' Mel looked up and was surprised to see Cyril reading from another book, a book about adolescence.

'Your Highness, I must insist you put that book down, please!' Mel requested, somewhat agitated.

Cyril dropped the book, blushing.

'With all due respect, Your Highness, I would like to know if you were paying attention.'

'Yes,' said Cyril. 'The monkeys, the volcanoes, the hard

beaches and the…adaptability.'

Mel paused. 'Very good, Your Highness.'

'I just find it hard to believe that we are related to those monkeys,' said Cyril.

'Oh, indeed,' said Mel. 'We have forward-facing eyes, on a relatively flat face, hands with thumbs and large brains for our body size. We also have a vertical spine which connects to our skulls from underneath, rather than from behind like most other animals. By the way, did you know that nothing on our body is just for decoration?'

'How interesting,' murmured Cyril. 'You know, I'm feeling rather peckish after learning all these new things.'

'May I offer you a biscuit or a cucumber sandwich?'

'No, thank you. I've got some money. I'll go to a café or restaurant.'

'Perhaps you could visit Lydia's inn,' suggested Mel.

Cyril was intrigued. 'Lydia's inn? Who…?'

Inside Prince Matthias's tree, the King and Queen were strolling through the great hall with Matthias. The hall was lined with concrete pillars, and a single strip of red carpet lay on the floor for them to walk along, since the walls and much of the floor were made up of the actual tree itself. The hall was decorated with the tree's own green leaves growing out from the walls, and there were numerous tunnels that the tree had been specially grown to form.

Matthias, dressed in white tights and a long, purple coat, may have been less majestic than his older brother, the King, but he was much more cheerful, with his bright smile and mop of dark, curly hair.

'And here are the statues of some of our ancestors,' he said, as wooden sculptures began to surround them on both sides of the walkway.

'This hall truly smells of repellent,' said the King. 'You must use an awful lot.'

'Well, there are so many snakes and rodents about,' shrugged Matthias. 'And it's also easily absorbed by the wood, isn't it?'

'Does anybody else think we should perhaps move on to luncheon?' asked the Queen, with only the slightest hint of urgency.

'Of course, my love,' said Matthias. 'Come, let us eat.'

They took a right turn onto the next walkway then passed through a leafy, wooden archway, coming to a stop at a grand table surrounded by chairs.

'Please, make yourselves comfortable, I'll be back in just a moment,' said Matthias as he headed towards the kitchen.

The King and Queen sat down at the table and the Queen began to wring her hands anxiously. She still felt guilty for leaving their home whilst Cyril was out.

'Don't you worry,' said the King, taking her hand. 'Cyril will be fine.'

'It's not Cyril I'm worried about,' said the Queen. 'At least, not *just* Cyril.'

'It's alright, I know we didn't travel here as quickly as we could have done,' said the King. 'But I'm sure we can work out a quicker route home, we just need to think.'

Cyril was sitting by himself, at a table at Lydia's inn.

The inn was an old building, with cream-coloured inner walls, a frame of wooden beams and dark, varnished floorboards. There were people sitting at the tables around Cyril and he had started up conversation with a few of them.

'No, my parents aren't with me today,' he explained to two jolly young men in large, casual, dark coats.

Both men were quite small, with pointy ears.

'Is this your first outing alone then, Your Highness?' asked a lady with two children, also dressed in casual clothing.

'Yes,' said Cyril. 'Well, certainly beyond the garden wall anyway.'

He turned round to see Lydia, the owner of the inn, standing in front of him.

Lydia was as straight as a sunflower, having reached adulthood a few years ago, and she carried herself with an elegance that made her maturity evident. Her dark hair was tied back securely behind her pointy ears and her two horn-like head crests, and her dark dress and black waistcoat were accompanied by contrasting white sleeves, which covered not just her arms but her tail as well. To emphasize her yellow eyes, she wore a yellow ribbon round her slender neck. She was holding Cyril's lunch, consisting of a pastry pie surrounded by greenery, and a glass of wine.

'Your order, Your Highness,' she said, in her silvery voice.

She placed the tray on Cyril's table and sat down beside him.

'Is something the matter?' asked Cyril, slowly, unsure why she had decided to accompany him.

'Please, go ahead and eat while I talk with you, Your Highness,' said Lydia reassuringly.

Cyril started eating as Lydia continued talking.

'I have, funnily enough, encountered Your Highness up close before, or so my parents tell me. When you were about half a year old, you were brought to my father's restaurant to visit the public for the first time. Actually, it was the second time, just after the royal baptism. I was a toddler and, well…'

'Yes?'

'I have something that we think belongs to you.' Lydia held out her hand and presented a clean, white handkerchief.

'Why, that's just a handkerchief,' said Cyril.

'Your Highness…'

'Oh, you can just call me Cyril.'

'You dropped this as a baby and I anticipated that you just might turn up here someday,' said Lydia. 'So, I've kept it safely hidden, ever since that day.'

Cyril held out his hand and Lydia delicately placed the handkerchief in his palm. To his surprise, she held onto his hand for a moment longer, speaking quietly.

'Most people think it unnatural for a young woman to be working these long dayshifts. Honestly and truly…Cyril, what are your thoughts?'

Cyril did not know what to tell her. His mind was blank.

'*Unnatural*…?' he began. 'I think…I think you

should…decide for yourself…maybe?'

'Are you feeling okay, Cyril?' asked Lydia, arching her back slightly and dropping her chin line.

'Yes…I'm just a bit tired, I think.' Cyril's hands were trembling.

'What have you been up to today then?' Lydia enquired.

'I've been learning about the coastal primates,' said Cyril.

'Oh, I should stay away from those if I were you,' advised Lydia, sitting up again. 'They're savage animals, very savage indeed.'

'As a matter of fact…' said Cyril, 'I've already been harassed by both species.'

Lydia gave Cyril an uncertain look.

'I met Mel Blue-Bottom and he told me that I'm an animal,' Cyril went on. 'I mean, I'm an animal, he's an animal, you're an…'

Suddenly, Cyril choked and looked in horror at Lydia's head crests. Lydia put her hands on the table as if she were about to stand up.

'Well, your lovely neck is clearly positioned under your skull like the rest of ours are,' said Cyril. 'But…your horns…I mean, crests….'

Lydia stroked one of her crests. 'Yes, what about them?'

'You have a tail as well, don't you?' asked Cyril.

Lydia lifted her slim tail, revealing the hairs on the end, which she proceeded to wave at Cyril.

'And are you a herbivore…I mean, a vegetarian?'

'Yes, how did you know that?' exclaimed Lydia. 'Do I look like one?'

'No,' said Cyril. 'Well, maybe, in a way.'

Lydia leaned slightly forward again. 'What is it, Cyril?'

'The West Coast primates!' exclaimed Cyril. 'They're vegetarians, like you…and they have tails, like you, and…head crests.'

'Like me?'

'Like you, Lydia,' confirmed Cyril.

'Yes, I am aware of that,' said Lydia. 'They're my ancient relatives.'

'Are they?'

'Yes, but that doesn't mean I'm fond of them.'

'You are one though,' said Cyril nervously. 'Could that mean that *I'm* also related to them, in some way?'

'Listen, Cyril,' said Lydia. 'You are obviously rather anxious. Why don't you return to the sanctuary of your home and think more about this?'

'I'll finish my lunch first then go for a walk afterwards, to clear my head,' said Cyril.

'Very well,' said Lydia, excusing herself from the table.

The King and Queen were finishing their lunch at Matthias's home with a delicious apple crumble.

'It has been nice dining with you, Matthias,' said the Queen as she stood up. 'Which is the quickest way back to our home?' she asked the King.

'Well, if we follow the river all the way to the mouth and stick to the east coast, it should speed up our journey by a good twenty minutes,' the King replied as he stood up too.

'Thank you for the meal,' said the Queen to Matthias, and she gave him a hug.

'You're welcome,' said Matthias. 'Are you in a hurry?'

'She just gets a bit stressed when Cyril's not with us,' assured the King.

'Well, send him my regards,' said Matthias. 'Do you remember your way out of here?'

'Yes, I think so.' The King ushered the Queen back through the arch, and they almost ran through the great hall as they quickly made their way out of the tree.

Just outside the city, Cyril and Finnegan came to a wooden bridge that crossed a ravine. They could see the city from the bridge where the river ran into it.

'Are you sure this bridge can take our weight?' asked Cyril.

'Maybe if we go over it one at a time,' suggested Finnegan.

A young lady suddenly appeared between them and the bridge, wearing a dark blue coat and tights, with her ginger hair tied back in a ponytail. She had pointy ears, like Lydia, but no tail, and Cyril thought she looked rather suspicious.

'Prince Cyril, is it?' she asked.

Cyril climbed off Finnegan.

'Yes, I am the Prince, but who are you?'

'I am E.V.,' said the lady. 'They're my initials. My full name is Emilia Varnish but it's a bit of a mouthful, don't you think?'

'Well, nice to meet you, E.V.,' said Cyril. 'Could we get

past please?'

E.V. hesitated. 'Before you do so, let me show you something.' She started looking through her pockets, and Cyril came over to her and put his arm round her.

'Are you up to something?' Cyril asked.

'Not just yet,' E.V. replied.

As Cyril lowered his arm, his hand ended up in one of E.V.'s pockets, and when he pulled it out it was covered in some kind of red liquid.

'What's this?'

'False blood, Your Highness,' explained E.V. 'I use it for practicing life-saving skills; that's what I want to show you…'

E.V. held up a certificate, which had apparently been awarded to her after completing a 'life-saving and survival training' course. As he took a closer look, Cyril accidentally put his finger to his mouth, smearing it with the false blood.

'I can give you a demonstration if you like?' offered E.V.

'No, thank you,' said Cyril. 'I've had enough trouble today.'

He walked back over to Finnegan and they headed back into the trees.

'Cyril?' said Finnegan. 'Wasn't that unwanted physical contact, putting your arm around her?'

'She's only an animal,' said Cyril. 'Definitely related to the thalassopithecus.'

'Still, your mother wouldn't want you to partake in that kind of contact, would she now?'

The King and Queen were cloaked up again and riding along the East Beach.

'Look,' exclaimed the Queen. 'Seals!'

Indeed, there were a few seals on the rocky part of the beach.

'They're just as much at home on land as they are in the water, aren't they?' said the King.

The seals suddenly hauled themselves away from the area, moving fast, as if wanting to run.

'I think I'll just take a brief look,' said the Queen, climbing off Gillian and slowly peering over a ledge.

The King climbed off Trevor and came up alongside her. 'What is it, love?'

Before they could say anything else, a silhouette climbed up in front of them. They froze.

By this time, Cyril and Finnegan had arrived at Matthias's tree.

'Ah, I have so many memories of this place,' said Cyril. 'Those hills and that lake haven't changed a bit. Well, at least, I don't *think* they have.'

'I can see a stable,' said Finnegan.

There was a stable right next to the main doors, and a few horses could just be seen moving behind the stable gates.

'They must be Boris and Caroline,' said Cyril, having climbed off Finnegan. 'We'll take a closer look, but we won't go in today, alright? Come on.'

Unbeknownst to Cyril, Matthias had been gazing out

of one of the windows of his tree and had spotted the young Prince and his horse as soon as they had arrived. As Finnegan and Cyril made their way to the gates, Matthias made his way down from the tree, and just as Cyril came to the bars of the gates, Matthias appeared to greet them. He gave his guards the sign to stand down.

'Hello, Cyril!'

The two of them shook hands through the bars.

'Hello, Uncle,' said Cyril.

'When did I last see you then?' asked Matthias.

'Oh, I don't remember,' said Cyril. 'I was quite young.'

'It's funny, your parents were here just a little while ago,' said Matthias.

'What did you say?' demanded Cyril.

'Your parents, they were here. They left about half an hour ago.'

Cyril looked enraged.

'What's wrong, Cyril?' asked Matthias, confused by his nephew's fury.

'Which direction did they go in?' said Cyril, through gritted teeth.

'Along the river towards the East Beach,' said Matthias.

'The East Beach!'

'They wanted to take a quicker route home and decided to go via the beach.'

'No!' exclaimed Cyril. 'There are monsters on that beach! I have to go and rescue them.'

After shaking Matthias's hand again, he jumped back onto Finnegan. 'Come on, Finnegan. Charge!'

As dusk fell, the King and Queen were trapped on the beach, being tormented by the thalassopithecus. Their hands and feet had been tied together and they had both been suspended from horizontal logs, as though they were about to be cooked alive. The creatures had also restrained Trevor and Gillian, binding them with lassos round their necks. Fortunately, they had not decided to roast the King and Queen yet; they were just having too much fun swinging them back and forth and playing with their sparkly crowns.

'You're making a big mistake!' cried the Queen. 'Just you wait until our son finds out about this!'

'Don't bother trying to get their attention now,' whispered the King. 'We'll break loose in a minute.'

The thalassopithecus suddenly turned as Lawrence Toadstool burst out of the trees on his horse. 'Oh, forgive me for being late, Your Majesties, but at last I've found you! Release those humans, immediately!'

The creatures chuckled but Lawrence and his horse, Sebastian, jumped onto the beach and rode quickly over to where the King and Queen were being held hostage.

Mr Toadstool is it?' said the Queen.

'Yes, Ma'am,' said Lawrence. 'It looks like I found you not a moment too soon.'

'How did you know where we were?' asked the King.

'Enough of the chitter-chatter,' interrupted a primate, standing in Lawrence's way.

At that moment, Cyril and Finnegan came hurtling out of the trees.

'Take this, you monsters!' screamed Cyril, throwing a

burning pinecone onto the sand.

It frightened the primates at first, but the tide soon covered it, and the tribe began to advance once more. Thinking quickly, Cyril and Lawrence set alight more pinecones, throwing them forcefully at the creatures.

Eventually, all the thalassopithecus had been scared away, disappearing into the trees and the water.

'Didn't you say that your mother told you never to play with matches, Cyril?' asked Finnegan.

'She did,' Cyril replied.

'She obviously never told you not to play with other types of wood though,' laughed Lawrence.

'Hey!' yelled the King. 'The tide's coming in!'

He and the Queen were still restrained, so Cyril and Lawrence went over to help them, untying their bonds and helping them over to a rocky ledge to recover. The King and Queen's crowns had slipped into the wet sand, but their horses, Trevor and Gillian, picked them up with their teeth and carried them over to the rocky ledge.

The Queen's hair was in a bit of a mess, and she was exhausted and ashamed. She sat next to Cyril, holding his hands.

'I'm truly sorry we had to leave our home, Cyril.'

'Really,' said Cyril. 'You warn *me* not to tell lies and…'

'I know, I know, Cyril,' said the Queen. 'Will you forgive us?'

Cyril gave a resigned sigh. 'I suppose so.'

The Queen hugged him as the horses appeared with the crowns, giving them to the King and Queen.

'So, how did you know where we were?' the King asked

Lawrence.

'I think Your Majesty should ask Cyril about that,' said Lawrence. 'He told me that those creatures had captured his parents on the East Beach, or something along those lines.'

'Oh, yes…I did, didn't I?' said Cyril, surprised. 'As it turns out, they had.'

As he stepped back, he caught sight of something behind the ledge. He peered over to get a closer look, and saw a tired looking thalassopithecus, covered in bumps and bruises. It was lying down and, as Cyril moved closer, it crawled away, slithering into the sea.

'Is there something there, Cyril?' asked the Queen.

'Just an injured primate,' said Cyril, as he came back to sit on the ledge. 'It was badly wounded. I wonder who could have done that.'

'We did,' said the King.

'What?'

'It was our…animal instinct,' said the Queen. 'We were just trying to defend ourselves.'

'And you told me not to use unwanted physical contact,' said Cyril, glaring at them both.

The Queen stood up. 'Now, now, Cyril. You've had a tiring day. What's that by your mouth?' She caught sight of E.V.'s false blood on Cyril's face.

'Oh, that,' said Cyril, automatically. 'I um…I used physical…no…I mean…'

'I understand,' said the Queen. 'You must have stormed rather roughly through that forest. Let me kiss it better for you. After all, it's the one time you approve of kissing.'

'Oh…if you must…' said Cyril, uncomfortably, as she kissed him.

'So, you know about the thalassopithecus, Your Highness?' said Lawrence to Cyril.

'Yes,' said Cyril. 'And the australophotherium.'

The King and Queen exchanged confused looks.

'I spent all day learning how those animals came to live here and there,' Cyril went on. 'I asked Mel Blue-Bottom and he told me. I also met some other people and was just fascinated by how we're all related. One interesting giveaway to our relationship with those creatures is our vertical spines.'

He put his hand on the back of his mother's neck and continued. 'In primates, the spine connects to the skull vertically, but in other animals it connects horizontally. Isn't that fascinating?'

'Well, Your Highness,' said Lawrence.

'Cyril,' said the Prince.

'Cyril. You have been learning a great deal about the world, haven't you?' said Lawrence. 'I would have gladly told you myself and saved you a lot of time, as I am a natural historian. But you were clearly too anxious to save your dear parents, weren't you?'

'Yes…' said Cyril, slowly, as the Queen hugged him again. 'Not quite the truth,' he thought to himself.

'Would you like to learn more about the world and its animals?' said Lawrence.

'Yes, please,' said Cyril. 'Why not? I'm beginning to see the world more realistically now.'

Cyril's parents then gave each other satisfied glances.

'I can take you out every so often and guide you through the natural world,' said Lawrence. 'I have carrier pigeons and could always send messages to you.'

'A splendid idea, Mr Toadstool,' said the Queen. 'We'll make arrangements, but right now I'm sure we are all extraordinarily weary. How does the day after tomorrow at the gates of the city sound?'

'At lunchtime maybe,' said Lawrence.

'That's settled, then,' said the Queen.

With that, the royal family and Lawrence gathered up their horses and climbed onto them.

'You will be doing us a great favour, Mr Toadstool,' said the Queen to Lawrence.

'I will not let you down, Majesties,' said Lawrence.

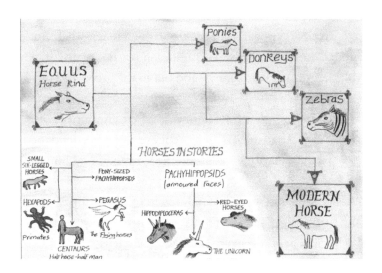

CHAPTER II
NOBLE STEEDS

It had been a week since the King and Queen made their arrangement with Lawrence Toadstool, and they had sent carrier pigeons back and forth. Today was the day when they'd agreed to give Cyril his first expedition and they were expecting Lawrence while they ate their breakfast.

It was a chilly day with white sky. The King was wearing his usual robe and the Queen had put a shawl on. Cyril however wasn't even wearing his scarlet coat.

'Aren't you a little cold, Cyril?' asked the Queen.

'Not really,' said Cyril.

'You will wrap up warm, won't you?' asked the King.

'Yes, I've got a cloak and scarf ready.'

Reginald appeared in the doorway. He was their butler and certainly had the tall and slender figure for it. His black uniform made him stand out in the green and brown chamber.

'Majesties, Your Highness,' he announced. 'Mr Lawrence Toadstool is here, requesting your attendance.'

'Thank you, Reginald,' said the Queen. 'Send him right in.'

As Reginald went to fetch Lawrence, the Queen spoke to Cyril. 'Remember, Cyril, you must be on your best behaviour, and do exactly as Lawrence tells you.'

'Yes, Mum,' replied Cyril.

Reginald returned to the dining room with Lawrence, ushering the scholar inside.

The King and Queen stood up as Lawrence entered. His cheeks were red from the cold and he was wearing a large, dark coat, pulled up around his neck.

'Wait here for a moment, Cyril,' said the Queen. 'We just need to have a word with Lawrence.'

Leaving Cyril to finish off his breakfast, the King and Queen swiftly left the room, with Lawrence in tow. Once they had walked far enough down the corridor to be out of earshot they stopped and Lawrence stood still, listening, as the King and Queen spoke to him, pacing all the while.

'We do appreciate your offer to take our Cyril out to see the world, Mr Toadstool,' said the Queen. 'But before we allow you to do so, we need to tell you a little more about him.'

'Of course, Your Majesty,' said Lawrence. 'Please, do tell....'

'We are simply concerned that Cyril may be difficult to teach,' the King explained. 'Ever since he was an infant, he has always been happy at the least-expected times.'

'We regret to admit that he often appears amused by other people's downfalls, though he does show sympathy every so often,' said the Queen. 'If he insists on moving on from what you have planned, I suggest you do not keep him waiting for too long.'

Lawrence's mind began to whirl. 'I shall do my best.'

The Queen smiled gratefully, and the King shook Lawrence's hand, before the three of them walked back to the dining room. Cyril stood up as they entered.

'Now, Cyril,' said Lawrence. 'If I may call him that...' He quickly turned to the King and Queen, who nodded. 'Today, we are going to study members of the horse family, by visiting the centaurs and unicorns.'

'Do you want to show Lawrence the way to the stable, Cyril?' prompted the Queen.

'Yes, Mum,' said Cyril.

He took Lawrence over to a solitary wooden door and opened it, revealing a staircase which led down to a gloomy passage.

Cyril started making his way down, but Lawrence hesitated, turning to the Queen. 'Like I said a while ago, Madam, I will not let you down. I promise.'

The Queen nodded and Lawrence followed Cyril down the stairs, closing the door behind him.

Cyril and Lawrence were soon in the back garden, preparing their horses Finnegan and Sebastian, and introducing them to each other.

'Are you the horse Lawrence was riding on, that time when we rescued Cyril's parents?' Finnegan asked Sebastian.

'Yes,' said Sebastian. 'I still say I could have frightened those monsters off easily.'

'But could you have done it whilst stuck in that quicksand?'

'Now, that will do,' interrupted Lawrence. 'Those monsters you keep talking about are our distant relatives, and today we are going into the mountains to visit some of *yours*, so you had best mind your manners.'

'He means the centaurs and unicorns,' explained Cyril.

'We'll be observing the centaurs to start with,' said Lawrence.

'Good,' said Cyril, as he wrapped his long cloak and scarf around himself. He had left them in the stable the day before, ready for today's adventure.

'Even though it's chilly right now, it's likely to brighten up this afternoon,' said Lawrence.

They walked their horses round to the main gate but had to go through the garden in order to do so, as work was being done round the other side. The royal guards, who were also dressed in warm cloaks, greeted them, and opened the gate. Cyril took a breath of fresh air, looking out at the rock formations and trees that surrounded his home.

'Okay then, Cyril,' said Lawrence. 'Let's get started.'

They both mounted their horses, and set off, riding in the direction of the centaur territory.

After a trek of some distance, they came to a dense forest of tall trees.

'How are we supposed to find anything in these parts?' Cyril remarked.

'Well, for a start, animals can't grow very big in this part of the forest,' said Lawrence. 'It's too restrictive. They can grow much bigger through there, where that light's coming from.'

Some small, horse-like creatures suddenly crossed their path, quickly disappearing into the ferns.

'What were those things?' asked Cyril.

'Hexapod horses,' said Lawrence.

Cyril looked confused, so they climbed off Finnegan and Sebastian, and Lawrence produced a small handbook.

'This manuscript contains information about all the world's animals. There are the common animals that you know, like horses, cows, elephants, tigers and so on, and there are those animals you might only have heard of in stories, like dragons, phoenixes, and of course, centaurs and unicorns.'

'Yes, but those…hexapod horses…' said Cyril. 'Didn't they have more than two pairs of legs?'

Lawrence opened the book and fanned through the pages. 'Yes, here they are. Originally, horses were small, about the size of a pet cat. They lived under the cover of trees and even learned to climb them. As a result of this breakthrough, they ended up growing an extra pair of legs and fingers. Some of them stayed in the forest, and remain here to this day, living like monkeys.'

'That's them, isn't it?' said Cyril. 'The hexapods we just saw?'

'Yes, they're not very well-known. Their hexapedal design eventually developed to fit the body proportions of the centaurs. The centaurs are half-horse, half-human. As the hexapods moved out into the open space, their descendants grew larger, straightened up, and their front legs turned into arms. They also developed more human-like skulls. The hexapod horse is what we call a missing link, the animal in between, as they have the feet of a small horse but the hands and head of a centaur.'

'Gosh,' said Cyril, looking at the book. 'It does sound complex.'

'This diagram is called a 'family tree',' explained Lawrence. 'Because it resembles the branches and shape of a tree. Everything in the Animal Kingdom is part of a family tree.'

Cyril took a moment to absorb the information and then he nodded.

'Let's move on,' Lawrence suggested.

They moved onwards still on foot and came to the opening at the other end of the forest, where a series of undulating hills stood, surrounded by trees and a large lake. On the grass stood a herd of centaurs.

Cyril was fascinated. 'They're just like they are in storybooks, but less colourful, and perhaps more graceful. What are those things around their shoulders?'

'Bows and arrows,' said Lawrence. 'Horses eat plants,

but primates are omnivorous, eating both meat and plants. Since centaurs are half-horse, half-human, they need a bit of both.'

Two centaurs appeared in front of Cyril and Lawrence as they climbed to the top of one of the hills. One was clearly male, with dark, curly hair, a strongly built chest and muscular arms, whereas the other appeared more feminine, with longer, straight hair and a smoother, curved body.

'What the…?' exclaimed Cyril, stepping back alongside Finnegan. 'I didn't want to get *this* close.'

'It's okay,' said Lawrence. 'They don't eat humans. They're very majestic animals, like you, Cyril.'

'Cyril?' said the male centaur. 'Is this young adult Prince Cyril?'

'Yes,' said Lawrence. 'This is the first time he has ever seen a centaur in the flesh.'

Cyril stepped forwards, where the beasts could see him.

'Oh, he is all grown up, even though his hair and complexion still resemble a darling young infant,' smiled the female centaur.

Cyril noticed something hiding behind the female centaur's legs. He whispered to Lawrence, 'Is that a baby?'

'Yes,' whispered Lawrence. 'Or a foal in this case.'

The mother guided her baby out from under her body, and the baby tilted its face upwards as Cyril bent down to get a closer look. It was a sweet looking thing, and Cyril had to restrain himself from crouching down and cuddling the little foal.

'You realise, Cyril, that centaurs have a double system?'

said Lawrence.

Cyril stood up straight again and looked at Lawrence in confusion. 'What are you talking about?'

Lawrence opened his handbook again as Cyril came round to look at it. There was a picture of a centaur's skeleton.

'You see, the centaurs have an extra set of ribs, containing an extra pair of lungs and an extra heart, in the horse half of their body. They are brave creatures, but anything with a double system would be, wouldn't it? That's probably the reason why they're so willing to hunt.'

Cyril looked at the centaurs and then drew his attention to the mountains in the distance behind them. 'Are we going over to those mountains now?'

'Yes, we are,' said Lawrence, closing the book. 'We'll have to go down this hill and across that green to get there though.'

Carefully, Cyril and Lawrence strolled down the hill with their horses, through the rest of the herd, with their two centaur acquaintances escorting them.

'Do you spend your time anywhere else?' Cyril asked the centaurs.

'Yes, Your Highness,' said the father. 'We need to travel far and wide to hunt for various foods.'

'We often visit the coast,' said the mother. 'But we've never been out to sea.'

'I don't know why you'd want to go out to sea,' said Cyril. 'But perhaps I could have it arranged for you, someday.'

They climbed up a stony slope, to the mouth of a huge

valley.

'Right then, we can carry on from here ourselves I think,' said Lawrence.

'Goodbye, and thanks,' said Cyril to the centaurs.

'You're welcome, Your Highness. If you ever need a favour involving perilous missions, most of us would be happy to assist.'

Cyril shook both the centaurs by the hand, and they smiled at him warmly, before turning back to the herd, leaving the mountains to Cyril and Lawrence.

'As we go through these mountains, we'll find more members of the horse family, and get to see how they behave in their natural habitat,' said Lawrence, pointing to the valley before them which consisted of brown hills, mist and an assortment of small streams.

Cyril climbed back onto Finnegan, Lawrence mounted Sebastian, and they began to journey deeper into the mountains.

Back at the tree, the King and Queen were sitting on their back patio drinking tea. The weather was beginning to get brighter.

'When were we last concerned about something other than Cyril?' asked the Queen.

'It must have been when we went to Matthias's,' said the King. 'And even then, he was still at the back of our mind.'

'Cyril has never been one to worry, has he?' the Queen mused. 'He knows little of fear. He always seems so brave…but there is a difference between brave and foolish, and I worry that he may be the latter.'

'Most animals have a sense of fear,' said the King. 'Not to mention the potential to protect members of their own kind. It's in their nature…you don't suppose *we're* animals, do you?'

The Queen turned round and looked up at their great tree. 'I wonder whether Lawrence may be right about that. We do have the same instincts, you're quite right.'

She then paused and the King turned to see what had caught her attention. The trees beyond the back gate were making a rustling sound, as if something were trying to ram its way through them. As the rustling drew nearer the back gate, the King and Queen stood up and ran down the steps that connected the patio to the garden below. They hurried past the hedges and flower beds, trying to gauge what was going on beyond the palace walls. Two guards came to the gates as the King and Queen reached them.

'Remember, do not attack until we can see who or what it is,' the Queen reminded them.

She and the King slowly peered through the bars as the rustling continued. Finally, one of the culprits appeared out of the trees.

'It's a unicorn,' said the Queen in amazement.

The unicorn in question had a light brown hide and her eyes seemed slightly unfocused.

'Greetings,' said the Queen. 'Are you quite well?'

She held out her hand and stroked the unicorn's muzzle, but the unicorn swung her head away. Three more unicorns appeared out of the trees and came up to the gates. They looked fierce.

'Our friend is blind,' said a sandy coloured male, with a brown mane.

'We don't need anyone else to interfere,' said another male, his vibrant red hide ragged from running through the trees.

'Please do not misunderstand, I was merely considering her well-being,' the Queen reassured them.

'Are you lost?' asked the King.

At that moment, the King and Queen's horses, Trevor and Gillian, along with another of their horses, Elizabeth, broke their way out of the stable and thundered down the hill. The King, Queen, and guards jumped out of the way as the horses slowed down and came to a halt at the gates. They began to exchange mumbling sounds with the unicorns.

'What are they doing?' whispered the King to the Queen.

'Communicating, I presume,' said the Queen. 'They must feel more comfortable among other members of their family. Why don't we invite them in?'

'What?'

'If they've made friends with our horses, the least we can do is let them stay here for a while,' said the Queen.

She nodded at one of the guards, who proceeded to open the gate cautiously, before beckoning the unicorns inside. All four unicorns nervously made their way into the garden.

'That was a good decision, Ma'am,' the Queen's horse, Gillian, said to her.

The Queen smiled. 'Now, I would like to prepare you all a drink and something to eat on the other side of the tree where there is plenty of space. As it happens, our servants are currently replacing the water pipes that run underneath that side of the hill, meaning we shall have to go round via the garden. Follow me, please...'

Having successfully made their way through the mountains, Cyril and Lawrence had come to a field of small hills on the edge of a forest. They could see the city in the distance, but before the city was a herd of pony-sized unicorn-like creatures, running about wildly where Cyril and Lawrence could see them.

'Are they unicorns?' Cyril asked, curiously.

'Some of them, yes. They are miniature members of the unicorn family.' Lawrence showed Cyril another page in his book. 'All creatures in the 'thick-faced horse' family are known as pachyhippopsids, and then each creature within that family has its own name. Unicorns have only one horn, but see these ones with two horns? They're called hippodiploceras. They lock each other's heads together with their horns when they fight.'

'Fight?'

'Rutting is the technical term. All pachyhippopsids rut, but only hippodiploceras lock horns. Look, two of them are doing it right now!'

Cyril looked over to where Lawrence was pointing and sure enough, two of the little animals were indeed rutting.

'Now, do you see those black horses with the head-crests over there?' said Lawrence. 'Those are called red-eyed horses, or red-eyed ponies in this case. Like australopotherium, they turn their crests red to create an attractive colour display, which they use when they're rutting. All these miniature pachyhippopsids have larger relatives; they're basically the same animals, only horse-sized rather than pony-sized.'

'Does that mean there are large unicorns about too?' asked Cyril excitedly. 'I would really like to meet them.'

'Yes, well, they're quite dangerous,' said Lawrence. 'And I promised your parents I'd take care of you. They're back there somewhere, high in the hills, but—'

'Look, the small ones are moving away!' Cyril exclaimed.

And they were. The herd was continuing their walk over the hills, heading towards the city.

'We'll just have to follow them, slowly and quietly,' said Lawrence.

With Finnegan and Sebastian following them, they began to stalk the animals over the hill. As they followed the herd into a ravine, they caught sight of E.V.'s bridge.

'They've come down to the river to drink, haven't they?' said Cyril.

E.V. suddenly appeared in front of them.

'Hello, Your Highness.'

'Oh no, not you,' sighed Cyril.

'What's wrong?' said Lawrence. 'This is E.V. and she's been trained in the art of survival.'

'I know that,' said Cyril. 'But my life doesn't need saving right now, and I'm not sure I trust her.'

'I tell you what, I'll give you both a glass of wine, to

show you that I bare no ill will.'

E.V. took out a small bottle of wine and two glasses from her coat, and she filled the glasses with the wine. She handed the first glass to Lawrence and held out the second to Cyril.

'My parents rarely let me drink alcohol, but I'm sure one glass won't hurt.' Cyril took the glass from E.V. and gulped it down. 'Hmm, an interesting taste. Thank you.'

They both gave the glasses back to her.

'Well, we should get a move on,' said Cyril.

'Yes, let's,' Lawrence agreed.

As they turned to Finnegan and Sebastian, their bodies went cold, everything went numb and they both dropped to their knees.

'Lawrence, what's happening to us?' Cyril cried. 'It feels like we've been poisoned!'

'I should have listened—' Lawrence was cut off as they both fell to the ground and passed out.

E.V. appeared horrified. 'Goodness, what's happened? Don't worry. I'll bring you round in a moment!'

She knelt down next to them and started talking to herself as if trying to remember something. Then she slapped her hand back and forth across their faces, in a futile attempt to wake them up. It didn't work. She knocked their heads together, but that didn't work either. Finnegan and Sebastian were having none of it.

'She's not very bright, is she?' said Finnegan.

'It looks as though something might have happened in her life which affected her state of mind,' Sebastian remarked.

They trotted over to E.V., who immediately turned to look at them when she saw their shadows approaching.

'E.V., do you realise who you are dealing with there?' said Finnegan. 'That is in fact the Prince of the realm.'

'Yes, I know,' said E.V. 'I invited him for a drink, did I not?'

'You must have forgotten how to awaken them,' sighed Sebastian. 'Finnegan?'

The two horses pressed their hooves down on Cyril and Lawrence's stomachs, and after a few moments, the Prince and his companion coughed and sat up.

'What…happened?' asked Cyril.

'You got drunk,' said E.V.

Cyril still felt cold in the centre of his body. He lifted his shirt and saw that his tummy was blue…and so was Lawrence's!

'It seems that wine contained blue dew,' said Lawrence. 'It's a plant that will turn your tummy bright blue if you ingest it.'

'It won't stay blue for long,' E.V. assured them. 'Only a few hours.'

'Oh great, thanks,' muttered Cyril. 'Come on, Lawrence.'

They slowly walked Finnegan and Sebastian away, in the direction of the herd of unicorn creatures, taking no notice of E.V. behind them.

'If you need help again, just let me know!' she called.

'She must have been involved in some kind of life-threatening situation, which left its mark on her mind,' explained Lawrence to Cyril.

'So, a serious accident damaged her brain, then?' said Cyril.

'It's the most likely reason, especially when you consider what she's been trained in,' Lawrence shrugged.

'But why hasn't she seen a doctor?'

'Well, the memory loss may not have been noticeable to begin with. It may have developed over time, slowly becoming more and more of a problem,' suggested Lawrence. 'We should let somebody know about it as soon as we can.'

Meanwhile, the King was guiding the blind unicorn onto the open green, around the side of the hill. The other unicorns and horses were already there, standing and talking while a meal was being prepared for them. With the assistance of their gardener Nancy, the Queen, with her sleeves rolled up and her crown off, was filling a trough with horse feed and with apples from their greenhouse.

'So, Dora?' said the King to the blind unicorn.

'Yes,' Dora, the blind unicorn, replied.

'And Ernest?' said the King to one of the male unicorns.

'Yes,' said Ernest.

'Dora, Ernest, Jessica, Benjamin, Looney, Dopey, Crazy...' The King stopped. 'No, wait, I'm going through the list of nicknames I used to give Cyril when he was toddling!'

'Please, enough with that old humour,' sighed the Queen, as she and Nancy carefully lifted the full trough and began to carry it over to the gathering of horses and unicorns.

'Okay, there we are,' said the Queen. 'We're going in for our lunch now. Nancy here will remain in the garden to keep an eye on you.'

'Please, dig in,' encouraged the King.

The horses and unicorns eagerly obliged, tucking into their feast. The King and Queen stopped for a moment to watch them from the bottom of the steps.

'Cyril would love to see this,' said the Queen. 'Do you think he'll be back before they leave?'

'I can't say,' said the King. 'Those unicorns still look somewhat hazardous to me.'

Having recovered from their earlier shock, Cyril and Lawrence were now stalking the herd of miniature equines up a hill, their horses trailing behind them.

'Why would they want to go uphill towards a forest?' asked Cyril, quietly.

'Maybe they just want to be left alone,' Lawrence replied.

As they approached the top of the hill, they noticed a strange-looking house. It was made of the usual wooden beams and cross-hatched windows, but the beams were red and purple and the walls black. Instead of smoke rising from the chimney, there was steam rising a short distance from the house.

'Oh, dear,' murmured Lawrence.

'What is it?' asked Cyril.

'That's the home of the three witches,' said Lawrence.

'They communicate well and are good cooks, but they can sometimes turn wicked. I just hope they don't harm the herd.'

Cautiously, Lawrence, Cyril and the two horses climbed to the top of the hill, staying low to the ground. Sure enough, when they reached the top, there were indeed three witches, standing just outside their strange hovel. They were all relatively young, wearing black robes and pointy hats. One of them, who had pointy ears, was ushering the last few members of the herd to the other side of the hill, away from their house. The other two witches were busy cooking, stirring a giant metal cauldron. One of the two cooks had a tail, and the other had pink eyes and was holding a recipe book.

'Leave the herd alone,' ordered the witch with a tail. 'They're not worth it.'

'Go and get those spices,' the pink-eyed witch demanded. 'This recipe could take a while.'

The pointy-eared witch rolled her eyes at them both and went into the house in search of the ingredients. Meanwhile, Cyril and Lawrence were crouching down by the top of the hill, so that the witches couldn't quite see them.

'We should go past one at a time,' suggested Lawrence. 'I'll whistle when I'm clear and ready for you to come over.'

'Okay,' said Cyril.

Lawrence, along with Sebastian, emerged from their hiding place and the witches turned to look at him.

'Afternoon, ladies,' he said jovially. 'What's cooking

today, then?'

'Nothing for the likes of you,' snarled the tailed witch. 'There's only enough for three to have this meal.'

'So, who's the third person?' asked Lawrence.

The two witches turned, to see that the pointy-eared witch was still in the house. A split second later, she emerged, carrying a wooden tub of ingredients.

'That looks like it's going to be quite the meal,' said Lawrence, looking at the spice-covered meat in the tub. The witches ignored him.

Cyril waited impatiently. 'What's taking him so long?' he whispered to Finnegan.

He peeked over the top of the hill. Once Lawrence finally reached the trees, he made his whistling sound and Cyril heard it, bringing Finnegan over to the other side of the hilltop. They too were spotted by the witches.

'Your Highness?' exclaimed the pink-eyed witch.

'Yes, I am Prince Cyril,' said Cyril.

'I'm delighted to meet you, Sir,' said the pink-eyed witch, holding out her hand for Cyril to shake. Cyril reached out his hand.

'Hey!' said the pointy-eared witch.

'What?' said the pink-eyed witch, turning round.

'Don't do it. We don't need fingers for this recipe.'

'We still need that blue dew,' said the tailed witch.

'I couldn't find it,' said the pointy-eared witch.

Cyril was shocked. 'I'll…just be off then.'

'I think His Highness had something to do with that blue dew of yours,' Finnegan remarked.

'Finnegan!' murmured Cyril sharply. 'Don't listen to

the horse. He's not worth it.'

The tailed witch came over and lifted up Cyril's shirt, revealing his blue tummy. 'Not worth it, eh?'

'So, can I get past, please?' Cyril asked nervously.

The next thing they knew, Cyril and Finnegan had been tied to a nearby tree and the witches were firing up a second cauldron.

'Why can't you keep your mouth shut, Finnegan?' said Cyril.

'Well, you remember what happened the last time you didn't confess, don't you?' said Finnegan.

'Quiet over there!' said the pink-eyed witch. 'Food can't talk.'

Lawrence was still hiding in the trees, and without being seen he sneaked up behind the tree to which Cyril was tied.

'Don't worry,' he whispered.

'Lawrence, thank goodness!' whispered Cyril.

'You didn't think I'd go on without seeing you safely across, did you?'

Lawrence began to untie them both.

'Aha!' cried the pink-eyed witch.

Cyril and Lawrence looked at her in horror, realising they had been caught.

'I suppose you have a blue underbelly as well, do you?' said the tailed witch.

'Yes,' said Lawrence, lifting up his shirt. 'And what's wrong with that?'

'You'll make an excellent addition to our lunch,' grinned the pointy-eared witch.

'Hang on a minute,' said the pink-eyed witch, looking in the recipe book. 'He's too old. Let's stick with the young Prince, he'll taste much better.'

'No, I'm bored of young meat, let's have a taste of something mature,' complained the pointy-eared witch.

'I say let's just cook the horse,' said the tailed witch.

'No, I want old flesh!'

'Well, I want young flesh!'

'Let's just have horse meat!'

The witches continued to argue back and forth, focused entirely on each other, giving Cyril and Lawrence the chance to slip away into the trees.

'They're clearly relatives of the thalassopithecus,' said Lawrence.

'Are they cannibals?' asked Cyril.

'Yes,' said Lawrence. 'But I have to admit, they do cook some delicious food.'

When they reached the other side of the hill and the edge of the forest, they noticed the herd of unicorn creatures down below.

'Is that the same herd?' Cyril asked.

'Yes, of course,' said Lawrence. 'They've been continuously eating the grass all this time. But that's what grazers do.'

'Speaking of eating, we haven't had our lunch yet.'

They sat down to eat their lunch, while Finnegan and Sebastian went to feed on the nearby grass.

'Hmm,' said Cyril. 'These sandwiches taste good. Where's the water?'

'Here…' Lawrence handed him a flask. Then he

opened the handbook again and turned to a page with information about the flying horses. 'Pegasus, as you may know, was the name of one particular horse in one particular story, but the species is known otherwise as the flying horse. They are horses, trying to be eagles. You might see some flying nearby. They often fly south at this time of year.'

'I thought I saw some giant birds above the mountains earlier,' Cyril remarked. 'I wonder what my parents would think of this.'

The King and Queen were enjoying a cup of tea and some biscuits on their garden swing, still talking to the unicorns.

'So, Dora, exactly how were you blinded, if that's not too personal a question?' asked the Queen.

'We often blind each other, Your Majesty,' said Dora. 'It's the result of fighting with a horn.'

'Why do you fight?' asked the King.

'It only seems like we're fighting from your point of view, Your Majesty,' said Ernest. 'Many other beings, including you yourselves, are surprisingly calm, I must say.'

The shadows were growing long, and the sunlight was beginning to fade.

'We should get a move on, fellas,' said Benjamin.

'Oh, but must you go?' said the Queen, standing up. 'Our son, Cyril, would very much love to meet you.'

'Apologies, Madam,' said Benjamin. 'But we are a desperate group of unicorns and have to keep track of the time of day.'

'You led the group when we came here, Benjamin,' interrupted Jessica.

'That was before Dora wandered off,' said Benjamin.

'You should let *me* lead,' said Ernest.

'I hadn't finished!' said Benjamin.

'A chance is a chance!' said Ernest.

'Who wants either of *you* to lead?' said Jessica.

Like the witches, the unicorns began fighting, but more physically and dangerously, as Dora's condition suggested. The horses as well as the King and Queen were stunned.

'I did tell you I was concerned about these animals,' recalled the King.

A short distance away, Cyril and Lawrence were back on their horses, travelling slowly along the steep ledge of a hill.

'It's getting late, Lawrence,' said Cyril. 'Are you sure this is the right way?'

'I can't afford to make a mistake like that, Cyril,' said Lawrence. 'Trust me. I know what I'm doing. It shouldn't be long now.'

After walking a bit further, they came to a house. It appeared to be made out of a giant toadstool; its dome-shaped roof was red with white speckles, and the stalk of the toadstool was incredibly wide and had windows.

'That's the house of Vincent Verccito,' said Lawrence.

'Who?'

'The artist. He designed some of the buildings in the city; he has a very vivid imagination.'

They continued round towards the front of the house and found a garden with a small white fence around it. On the patio sat an artist, whom Cyril assumed must be Vincent, painting at an easel. He had pointed ears, with ridges down them, and a tail, and he looked up from his work as Cyril and Lawrence approached.

'Good afternoon,' he said, standing. 'Can I help you?'

As Vincent walked towards the fence, he recognised Cyril and Lawrence, and once they had both dismounted from their horses, he shook their hands warmly.

'Your Highness,' said Vincent. 'I must say you've grown since I saw you last.'

'Oh, yes,' said Cyril. 'I've spent most of my recent years inside my tree.'

'We were just passing by on our way back there,' said Lawrence. 'We've been watching horses all day, haven't we, Cyril?'

'Well, now,' said Vincent. 'It's strange of you to say that, because I spotted a herd of unicorns not long ago.'

'Yes, we've been following them,' said Cyril.

'Really? It's not like the aristocracy to stalk a herd of deadly unicorns.'

'They weren't deadly, they were the size of ponies,' said Cyril.

Vincent showed them the painting he had been working on. It was a picture of a herd of large unicorns, against a darkening sky.

'Those are what I saw,' he told them.

'What a beautiful painting,' said Cyril. 'Where did the unicorns go after you saw them?'

'Can you see that valley over there?' Vincent pointed to some hills in the distance. 'That's your valley, Your Highness. I spotted the unicorns venturing over there.'

Cyril, without another word, scrambled back onto Finnegan. Lawrence followed.

'How bad could it be?' Cyril asked Lawrence.

'How bad could what be, Cyril?'

'Could the unicorns have broken into my garden and hurt my parents?'

'That's unlikely,' Lawrence reassured him. 'But we're nearly there, so we had best double check. Thank you for your time, Vincent.'

Night was creeping up on Cyril's home and it was beginning to rain. The King and Queen were sitting at the dining room table, while Reginald started lighting the candelabras.

'I just hope they haven't run into any danger.' The Queen had her elbows on the table and her head was bowed.

'Well, you did have Lawrence promise to take care of him,' said the King.

At that very moment, Cyril and Lawrence appeared through the door, the same door they had left through that morning.

'Oh, Cyril!' exclaimed the Queen, running towards her son, hugging him tightly and planting numerous kisses on his cheeks.

'You're trembling,' said Cyril. 'And what have I told you about kissing?'

'Oh, sorry, dear,' said the Queen. 'Thank you, Mr Toadstool. You've proven yourself most loyal.'

'I'm glad to be of service, Majesties,' said Lawrence.

'So, how was your adventure today, Cyril?' asked the Queen.

A few minutes later, they were all sitting at the table, listening to Cyril's account of the day.

'And then there were the unicorns,' he said.

'Oh, Cyril,' said the Queen. 'We must tell you...'

They told him about the unicorns and Cyril told them how dangerous Lawrence said they could be.

'One of the few exceptions to the urge of unicorns being aggressive towards people is when they catch them with horses, basically fellow family members,' Lawrence explained.

'Right,' said Cyril. 'But we had Finnegan...'

'I know we had Finnegan and Sebastian with us, but it was something I forgot about because I was busy thinking about your safety,' said Lawrence. 'It just slipped my mind.'

The Queen held Cyril's hand. 'I'm sorry you weren't here to see them, Cyril.'

'It is a shame,' said Cyril. 'But you know, it was interesting spending the day away from home, learning all the connections of the horse family. I'm looking forward to our next expedition.'

'It's good to know that, Cyril,' said Lawrence. 'Well, Majesties, I should be on my way now.'

But, just then, Cyril spotted something out of the window, in the sky. He could only see silhouettes, but they were definitely flying creatures.

'What are they?' he asked.

Lawrence turned to look. 'Goodness, that appears to be a flock of flying horses.'

The horses looked as though they were diving, swooping straight down into the garden.

'Oh, this I've got to see!' exclaimed Cyril, jumping up from his chair and running to the back door.

The King and Queen sighed.

'You wouldn't mind staying a little longer would you, Mr Toadstool?' asked the Queen.

It was still raining as Cyril flung open the back doors and ran down the steps, slowing as he approached the exotic horses. The garden was faintly lit by fluorescent, flat-headed toadstools that glowed green, indigo and purple, even in the rain, so he could just about see the animals, kneeling down on the grass. They were truly black beauties, and all had strange outgrowths on their heads.

'Hello!' exclaimed Cyril, enthusiastically.

'Oh, you must be the Prince,' said one of the horses. 'Are we on your lawn?'

'Yes, but don't worry. I want you to stay.'

In the meantime, the King and Queen had led Lawrence to the back doors, and they all came out to find Cyril chatting amiably with the horses.

'They certainly are flying horses,' said Lawrence. 'It looks like the Prince is persuading them to stay here.'

'Cyril!' called the Queen. 'We've already had a herd of unicorns in the garden today, we need to clean the lawn.'

'No, we don't, Mum!' said Cyril. 'You don't expect me

to miss my chance now, do you?'

The King, Queen and Lawrence sat down at the coffee table on the patio for a moment.

'He should be fine,' said Lawrence. 'Those horses have large crests; they're relatively harmless, most of the time.'

Cyril gazed in wonder as one horse turned its crest bright red. Lawrence, noticing the young Prince's amazement, wandered down the steps and over to Cyril.

'Just to let you know, Cyril, these horses, like the unicorns, can be aggressive if provoked. Everything seems to be working out for you so far, for which I am glad, but I just thought I ought to warn you to be careful.'

'Yes, yes,' said Cyril, paying little attention. 'This is great, isn't it? I even get to have my dinner served out here!'

Lawrence sighed internally. 'I'll see you in a month or so then, for another outing,' he reminded the Prince.

'Yes, see you then.'

As Lawrence bid the King and Queen goodbye, down by the main doors a few minutes later, he turned back momentarily to see Cyril enjoying his dinner, sheltering from the rain beneath the wing of a horse.

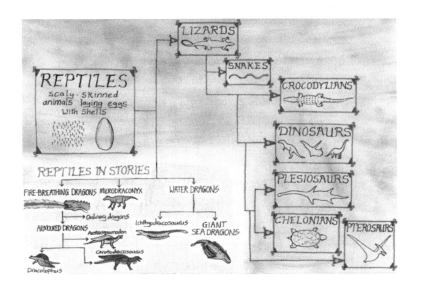

CHAPTER III

THE REPTILE KINGDOM

It was spring, and the garden was a haven of flowers and blossom covered trees. Cyril and his parents were on their back patio, drinking tea and waiting for Lawrence's arrival.

'You know, Cyril,' said the Queen. 'Some of the royal doctors think you might possibly have an issue with mood swings and the like. We love you very much, of course, but your father and I need you to try your best to be an honest, considerate person, alright dear?'

'Yes, Mum,' replied Cyril.

'If you are to rule a Kingdom one day, you have to be

in the appropriate state of mind,' said the King. 'It's not all roses and rainbows; you will have many duties that you need to perform in order to keep the public happy and safe. Ruling a Kingdom is a huge responsibility.'

The Queen put her hand on Cyril's wrist. 'Your people will see you as more than their master; they'll rely on you to provide protection as well. When making public decisions, you must first consider their expectations.'

'I think, for practice, I should have children first, perhaps,' mused Cyril.

'Perhaps,' said the Queen. 'One day, you will meet and marry a nice young woman and…well, I shan't say any more than that today. For a start, if things are troubling you, try to be honest and share your concerns with people. Don't keep them bottled up inside you.'

'Okay,' said Cyril.

'Lawrence will be here soon, so you can practice being considerate and responsible without us,' said the Queen.

Minutes later, Reginald appeared at the doors. 'Mr Toadstool has arrived to see His Highness.'

'That means you, Cyril,' whispered the Queen.

'Yes, I know,' said Cyril, standing up.

'Are you able to recognise people by their surname?' enquired the Queen.

'Yes, of course, Mum,' replied Cyril.

Lawrence appeared in the doorway and came onto the patio. 'Morning, Cyril.'

'It's getting warm, isn't it?' said Cyril.

'Yes, it is, just the weather for where I want to take you today.'

'And where's that?'

'The Reptile Kingdom,' said Lawrence.

The King and Queen looked worried.

'Ah, yes,' said Cyril. 'The home of lizards, dragons and snakes?'

'And much more,' said Lawrence. 'Now, this will be rather perilous, so I think it would be wise for us to carry those swords of yours.'

'Just go and wait at the gates, Lawrence,' said Cyril. 'I can see you've got our lunch. I'll go and fetch the swords and some snake repellent.'

He went back inside as the King and Queen walked Lawrence from the patio to the bottom of the steps.

'We've just been speaking with Cyril, Mr Toadstool,' said the Queen. 'And we want him to understand the responsibility of his possible royal future.'

'Yes, Ma'am,' said Lawrence.

'Whenever possible, please let him make some of his own decisions this time,' said the King.

'I am sure I do not need to remind you to be extra cautious about keeping him safe today though,' said the Queen.

'Well, today is all about taking the next step forward, is it not?' said Lawrence.

The Queen was looking tense but nodded in agreement. 'Precisely. Good luck.'

The King and Queen allowed Lawrence to make his own way to the main gates.

'Is something the matter?' the King asked the Queen. 'You're breathing a little heavily.'

'I just have a feeling we shouldn't be letting them venture into that territory,' said the Queen. 'But I suppose once shan't hurt.'

Later, in the South of the Kingdom, Cyril and Lawrence were on their horses, riding out over a hard open plain. It was very warm, and in front of them were a series of orange rock formations and canyons.

'So that's where the reptiles live?' said Cyril.

'Yes,' said Lawrence. 'They can only survive in a warm climate. In fact, rumour has it that the Reptile Kingdom is much bigger than it looks on all the maps. So much of the Reptile Kingdom has yet to be explored that we may have underestimated its size.'

'What exactly are reptiles?' asked Cyril.

'They're a group of animals that have scaly skin and lay eggs with shells. Their closest relatives are amphibians, animals which lay soft, see-through eggs and can live both in water and on land, like frogs for example.'

Cyril looked down and could see lots of small, green lizards, darting in and out of the horses' hooves. 'They're just like the snakes and lizards back at my tree.'

'Yes, well, grass-snakes and very small lizards seem to be able to live in cooler conditions.' Lawrence had opened his handbook. 'It's only the large reptiles, like crocodiles and boa constrictors, that rely on warmth. Many reptiles also need to keep their skin wet, which is why they are often found living in damp areas, such as swamps and rainforests. In fact, there are some thick and dangerous swamp forests just beyond those cliffs. Let's continue our journey; make sure Finnegan doesn't squash the lizards.'

'Why do I feel like we're being watched?' asked Cyril, nervously.

'Because there are buzzards that fly above this plain and patrol the coast,' said Lawrence. 'But don't worry, the only prey they kill and eat are those little lizards we keep almost standing on.'

'It's not very nice of them to do that, is it?' said Cyril.

'No, but sadly, Cyril, that's nature. Knowing that many animals stay alive at the expense of others, stealing their lives so to speak, helps you to understand that nature can be rather cruel sometimes.'

They could see a couple of birds circling above.

'Right,' said Lawrence, putting away the book. 'Swamp, here we come.'

It wasn't long before they reached the swamp forest, and Cyril and Lawrence dismounted their horses, deciding it was best to travel on foot. They began guiding their horses down the path, with Lawrence leading the way. The forest was dim, but there was sunlight shining through the trees from above. It didn't look too friendly; the trees were covered in ivy and there were lizards and frogs standing on rocks and branches, staring at Cyril and Lawrence as they walked by.

'I have a bad feeling about this place,' said Cyril. 'It's too quiet, and the heat is closing in around me.'

'Just keep following me, Cyril,' said Lawrence.

The four of them suddenly found themselves on the edge of a swamp. Strange shapes were moving through the green and black water, and the only way across was to walk along a line of stepping-stones.

'Right, Cyril,' said Lawrence. 'This is a test of nerves. Let's see just how well you can complete this slimy, gloomy obstacle course, shall we?'

'I'm not afraid,' said Cyril with confidence.

Very carefully, Lawrence led them over the stepping-stones. This was dangerous, especially for the horses, and they were about two thirds of the way across when a dark figure burst out of the water, grabbing Finnegan's leg.

'Finnegan!' screamed Cyril.

'Alligators!' cried Lawrence.

Sebastian tried to frighten off the alligator with his feet, but it was beginning to drag Finnegan into the water. Cyril took out his sword and quickly hopped across the stones to Finnegan.

'Let go of that horse!' he yelled, before jumping and stabbing the alligator through the skull as he landed.

He looked the monster in the eye until it lost its strength. Finnegan scrambled back onto the stepping-stones and Cyril, panting, held up his bloodstained sword. Sebastian was now able to support Finnegan and help him up onto the stones again. Finnegan's white ankle was stained by his own blood and he was limping. Lawrence put his hand on Cyril's shoulder.

'What…did I just do, Lawrence?' stuttered Cyril.

'It was your animal instinct,' explained Lawrence. 'You retaliated in order to save your loyal steed. I shouldn't tell your parents you did that, though.'

'Why not? Do you want to tell them?'

The swamp went surprisingly quiet all of a sudden and Cyril nervously held his sword over the water. He turned to see another alligator on the stones in front of them, and a third on the ledge on the other side.

Lawrence then took out his sword. 'More than one alligator...I was afraid of that.'

There were now alligators climbing up onto the stones behind the horses as well.

'Help!' cried Cyril.

But then there came a roar, and a long wooden spear plunged into the nearest alligator's front leg, frightening it back into the water. Cyril and Lawrence looked up to see a wild man-like being fly down from the trees onto the opposite side of the swamp. He landed on another alligator and quickly stabbed it in the back. Cyril and Lawrence quickly finished their way across the swamp, but Finnegan was still struggling and Sebastian was desperately trying to help him. Cyril, without a moment's hesitation, bravely came to the rescue, frightening off the remaining alligators. The horses at last made it across, but Finnegan was still limping.

The being who had just saved them had dark green skin, horns on his head and a necklace of bones around his neck; he looked very strong and heroic.

'Crikey!' said Cyril. 'I don't know what to say.'

The wild man said a few strange words and made a few gestures as he brought the two of them, with their horses, under the cover of the trees.

'Who do you two claim to be?' he then asked.

'Ah, well...' said Lawrence, as he and Cyril put their

swords away. 'I am Lawrence Toadstool and this is His Royal Highness, Prince Cyril.'

'Prince Cyril?' The wild man knelt.

'I am a dryoceratherium,' he said, as he stood up again. 'A horned inhabitant of the swamp forest.'

'I've heard of these people, Cyril,' whispered Lawrence. 'Little is known about them, but they don't appear to be too savage. What would you like to do now? We might be able to ask for help.'

'Okay, then,' said Cyril. 'Could you please take me to your civilisation if you have one?'

'That I can, Sir. That I can. Come...' The wild man took them deeper into the forest.

Whilst their son and Lawrence were venturing further into the Reptile Kingdom, the King and Queen were in their aquarium chamber, only in a different area, containing a multitude of thick plants and small reptiles. There were mirrors all around, making the greenery appear vaster, to try and ensure the little reptiles felt at home and to stop them climbing the roots of the tree.

'What if Cyril does find out?' contemplated the Queen.

'Really?' questioned the King. 'How could he?'

'There are savages in those disgraceful forests,' said the Queen, wheezing in panic. 'Supposing they have cave paintings? Or stone artwork on display? I shouldn't have let them go...I should not have let them go!'

She dropped onto her hands and knees and began to cry.

The King knelt down next to her and held her in his

arms. 'Just calm down, darling, you're over-reacting.'

'Our son…' sobbed the Queen. 'He may have Lawrence and their horses with him, but…we could have sent our own son into the jaws of death.'

'Please, you're making yourself ill,' said the King. 'Be strong…'

'I'm too strong!' exploded the Queen. 'I wish I'd never come into this royal family…' she moaned softly.

Their butler Reginald then came rushing down the stairs and into the chamber to see what had happened, and the King looked up.

'It's okay, Reginald,' he said. 'We're just having a moment.'

The dryoceratherium had brought Cyril, Lawrence and their horses to his tribe and their village, and Cyril and Lawrence were eating their sandwiches at a wooden table, talking to other members of the tribe. The buildings around them were made of wood and straw and decorated with bones.

'Well, this is certainly some adventure, isn't it?' said Cyril to Lawrence.

'I hope you don't get too comfortable, Cyril,' said Lawrence. 'We'll have to move on soon if we're to go any further and get back to your home before dark.'

Cyril understood, and after finishing his sandwich, he decided they should probably leave soon.

Finnegan and Sebastian meanwhile were resting under a tree. A witch doctor was treating Finnegan for his injury, pouring some kind of liquefied plant onto his wound.

Finnegan made loud noises but Sebastian was there to comfort him, like members of his own kind should.

After their owners came to fetch the horses, Cyril spoke with the wild man.

'Is there another safer way through the forest?'

'Yes, Your Highness,' came the reply. 'Should you take a left turn at the swamp on your way back, you will eventually come to a bridge of wood and rope. Once over the bridge, the danger will be over and you shall have a clear path back home.'

There were some moving shadows on the ground and they looked up to see a number of flying animals. They were much bigger than birds of prey and had wing membranes of skin rather than feathers.

'Those are flying pterosaurs!' said Lawrence. 'That means the dinosaurs aren't far away.'

'The dinosaurs?' said Cyril. 'There are dinosaurs here too?'

'Yes,' said Lawrence. 'We still have a lot to see, especially as the dinosaur family is so vast.'

'We'll go and see the dinosaurs in a minute,' said Cyril. 'Let's just see what our friend has to show us here first.'

The wild man then took them over to what looked like an exhibition. There were models and sculptures, made of bamboo and leaves.

'Do take a look at these pieces of artwork, Your Highness,' said the native, as he began presenting big leaves with paintings on them. 'They portray stories that have been told in these parts for many generations.'

He stopped when he came to a painting of a dragon

being slayed by a king.

'Say, that king there looks like my dad,' said Cyril.

'It is one of our more recent stories, Your Highness,' said the wild man. 'There are tales of a king, possibly your father, who once battled and defeated a fire-breathing dragon. Surely, he must have told you this?'

'I don't think he has,' said Cyril.

'In that case, Your Highness may take this item as a souvenir.' The native gave him the leaf.

'Thank you,' said Cyril. 'Do you know where to find the dinosaurs?'

'I do. You must walk a distance beyond those formations until you can hear the extraordinary animals. They are very loud and make a distinct sound – you will know when you have found them.'

Cyril and Lawrence looked to where the native was pointing. The cliffs awaited them.

As they continued their journey, with pterosaurs still flying high above, the landscape shifted yet again, becoming half-canyon and half-jungle.

'The dinosaurs shouldn't be difficult to find,' said Lawrence. 'They're big animals.'

They went down a path under the trees. Some agile animals came up running alongside and past them. They looked like flightless birds but like the pterosaurs they didn't have feathers, just scaly skin. When they finally emerged from the jungle, onto the edge of a hill, they found herds of dinosaurs scattered over the landscape in front of them.

'Oh, goodness!' exclaimed Cyril. There were so many different types of dinosaur, as Lawrence had said there would be. 'This territory must definitely be bigger than it appears on the map.'

Lawrence sat down on a rock with his handbook, and Cyril sat next to him, listening intently.

'Those giant, plant-eating or herbivorous dinosaurs, with long necks, are called sauropods, and are the largest land animals ever to exist, as far as we know. The ones with frills around their heads and horns on their faces, are called ceratopsians. They can turn their frills red for display and are also plant-eaters. See the bulky ones over there, with the pentagonal plates on their backs? Those are stegosaurs, again herbivores, but deadly, as they often use those four spikes on their tails to defend themselves against potential threats.'

Suddenly, there was a booming, thumping sound, making Cyril jump, and as the ground began to shake, some of the dinosaurs took cover. Cyril and Lawrence gazed down into the valley below to see a huge dinosaur head, with heavily built jaws and sharp teeth, thrashing through the trees.

'That's a Tyrannosaurus Rex!' said Lawrence. 'It's one of the biggest members of the theropod family, the only group of meat-eating dinosaurs.'

As soon as the carnivore ducked back down into the trees, they heard a series of rather horrible crunching noises.

'I don't like the sound of that,' murmured Cyril.

'At least you can't see it,' said Lawrence.

'*Not* seeing the horror is even more disturbing in some way,' Cyril shuddered.

'This may seem strange to you, Cyril, but did you know that the closest relatives of the theropod dinosaurs are actually birds.'

'Really?'

'Apparently. Some of those meat-eating dinosaurs have thinner bodies, longer necks, and smaller snouts, and look somewhat like an ostrich.'

'I see…' said Cyril. 'But, what about the feathers?'

'Oh, dinosaurs have feathers too. If you think about carnivorous birds of prey, such as eagles or hawks, you'll begin to see the resemblance, and the missing links.'

'I already can,' said Cyril. He turned his attention to the ragged cliff formations on the other side of the jungle. There were brooding, grey clouds beyond them; it did not look like the kind of sky that birds or even pterosaurs would want to fly through. 'Is that where the dragons live?'

'Yes. Now, Cyril, if we are to go and see the dragons, we can only watch them from the cliffs above, you understand? They are very dangerous.'

Cyril nodded, and Lawrence promptly packed away his handbook as they both mounted their horses. Then they headed down a jungle-covered slope, towards the cliffs, and into the dragon territory…

Before long, they found themselves on the shore of a lake, which lay beneath the most stable part of a cliff.

'Can you swim, Cyril?' asked Lawrence.

'Yes, fortunately I can,' said Cyril. 'I used to swim in my uncle's lake every summer. I'm more concerned about how shallow this water is than how deep it is.'

'Don't worry, we shouldn't need to enter the water at all, only if we need to make a sudden escape,' Lawrence reassured him. 'Come on.'

Dismounting their horses, and leaving them by the lake, Cyril and Lawrence cautiously began to climb the cliff. The temperature grew warmer, the sky darkening as they climbed higher, and they soon reached the top, sweating from exertion and the heat of the atmosphere. As they peered over the summit, they saw a large group of majestic looking, fire-breathing dragons, swooping through the air. In the distance, active volcanoes spluttered and rivers of lava oozed across the landscape. Many of the dragons were on the wing, but most of them were gathered together on the ground.

'There couldn't be anywhere much deeper and darker than this, could there?' Cyril observed, his eyes watering slightly.

Lawrence turned to a page in his book; there wasn't much light, but they could still just about see.

'Right, the ordinary dragons are these ones,' said Lawrence, pointing to one of the many diagrams.

'Some of them have horns, I think,' said Cyril, pointing to a spiky silhouette that was flying in front of a glowing, orange lava flow.

'Those are ceratodracosaurus,' said Lawrence. 'They have horns all the way down their backs, and even under their necks. When competing, they usually try and lock each other's necks together with their horns, wrestling with each other until one concedes or is too injured to continue.'

'Why do they live here, in such a boiling-hot environment?' asked Cyril.

'Mostly because there's more open space,' Lawrence explained. 'Besides, it's easier for large animals to make their way around the rivers of lava than it is for us. To hunt for food, they often fly over the sea to other volcanically-active islands.'

'Why is this area so volcanically active?'

'I'm not sure…most islands begin life as volcanoes and given that our mainland is surrounded by smaller islands, it makes sense to assume that we were once a tiny island too. Although we've grown, the volcanoes are still here. But come, let's focus on the animals for the time being. Competition and display are the speciality of dracolophus, those dragons with the head-crests and sails on their backs.'

'They do look rather unique,' said Cyril. 'With dragons like that, these lava fields could get pretty colourful.'

'Indeed. Then there are the austrasquamodon, named after the thick scales that cover every inch of their bodies.'

A shadow fell over them, followed by a loud thumping sound, causing the cliff to shake. They looked up. It was an austrasquamodon! The huge dragon bared its dagger-like teeth, staring at them with a chilling look in its fiery red eyes.

'Who are you and what are you doing here?' asked the dragon.

The creature's voice sent shivers down Cyril's spine.

'We don't want any trouble,' said Lawrence.

''Tis not polite to peek,' the dragon reprimanded them.

'We're sorry,' said Cyril solemnly. 'We didn't mean to spy on you.'

'Spy on us?' the dragon sneered. 'Who would be foolish and insolent enough to attempt such a thing? I have been combing these cliffs for some time now, in search of a particular dragon-slayer. No one can hide from me.'

'A dragon-slayer you say?' said Cyril. 'I think that might be my father.' He took from his pocket the leaf painting he had been given, and bravely presented it to the dragon.

'Your father, you say?' the dragon asked menacingly. 'You must be the Prince.'

'Yes, I am,' said Cyril. 'My father—'

'Your father…' interrupted the dragon, '…dared to murder my younger sibling. Since we were infants, I have wanted to hunt that slayer down and avenge my sibling. But now it seems I've found something better!'

The dragon scrambled towards Cyril, and he and Lawrence knew they were in serious danger.

'Now, Cyril!' shouted Lawrence.

They jumped off the cliff and plunged into the lake below, just seconds before the dragon's jet of fire hit the surface. The leaf painting drifted down and landed safely on the water. Cyril and Lawrence stayed under the water for a moment, just to make sure, before emerging cautiously. The dragon had flown away.

'That was close,' said Cyril.

'Too close,' Lawrence replied. 'Are you alright, Cyril?'

'Yes, I am, besides being soaking wet.'

They both laughed, relieved, and slowly sloshed their way out of the water. Once they had dried off a little, they made sure to dab strong snake repellent onto their coats, to keep any other potential predators away.

The King and Queen were in their throne room, talking with each other. The Queen was leaning wearily on the arm of her throne, her loosened hair and handkerchief in her hand making her look all the more bereft. The King handed her a goblet of wine.

'Thank you, dear,' she said.

'Where do you suppose he could be at this moment?' mused the King.

'I wish I knew,' said the Queen. 'I feel like I'm constantly holding my breath, spending the day in such agonising suspense like this. I shall not be able to sleep tonight until I know what has happened to Cyril. And he has three other souls with him, remember? Lawrence, and the two horses...they could be in danger too.'

'And they're constantly meeting more souls while they're out,' sighed the King. 'One of these days, they'll encounter one too many, if they haven't already. Hopefully, Cyril won't come back trying to fool us again.'

'You mean that time when he tore his clothes and deliberately cut himself to get out of trouble for being late?' The Queen stood up. 'No son of mine shall attempt that little trick more than once. He should know better by now. Come on, let us drink.'

They downed their wine, and the King promptly

poured them both another glass.

The sun was setting as Cyril and Lawrence walked their horses through the trees, back in the countryside of the North, and the sky matched the orange of Cyril's almost dry hair. As they looked down, they noticed a trail of footprints.

'Oh, dear,' said Lawrence, anxiously. 'I think I know what those footprints came from.'

'What?' Cyril asked.

Lawrence slowly turned his head towards Cyril. 'Miniature dragons. They're programmed to react to any noise made by a relative. In this case, they must have heard the austrasquamodon earlier and woken up. They normally come out at night, and hate being disturbed. We'd better be on guard, Cyril, in case they appear.'

'Alright,' said Cyril.

They climbed onto the horses and continued their journey back to Cyril's home. But as they proceeded through the forest, they heard rustling coming from behind one of the bushes.

'It's probably them,' whispered Lawrence.

They took out their swords, armed and ready for an attack; Cyril looked frightened but firmly held onto his sword. Then, without warning, three large, four-legged reptiles sprung out at them. Instantly, Finnegan and Sebastian reared up on their back legs, in an attempt to keep the creatures away from their riders. The tactic seemed to work as the reptiles stopped, apparently stunned into stillness. But Cyril and Lawrence were not out of danger yet, as the reptiles were clearly carnivorous, with their sharp teeth and strong legs. They needed to act quickly.

'I was right,' said Lawrence. 'They're called Microdraconyx, and they're powerful predators.'

Cyril didn't answer.

'We promise no harm will touch you,' said Lawrence to the miniature dragons. 'Can we help you?'

'Maybe you can…maybe you can't,' said one of the dragons, a brown one with horns on its face.

'Something is trying to hunt us down,' said another, a green dragon with hooked claws on its fingers and toes.

'We woke up to the noise of a savage monster,' said the third, which was grey and had a lumpy crest on its snout, and longer, straighter claws.

'That would have been a fire-breathing dragon,' said Cyril.

'Cyril…' hissed Lawrence, as the dragons looked in Cyril's direction.

'Those fire-breathers should learn to mess with somebody their own size,' remarked the horned dragon.

Cyril and Lawrence put their swords away.

'If you want to help, you can leave us in peace,' huffed the hooked-clawed dragon.

'Then leave you we shall,' said Lawrence.

Cyril nodded, and the dragons retreated into the forest.

'Let's turn away from this forest,' said Cyril.

They walked a little further and soon found themselves near the wall of the city, in front of E.V.'s bridge.

'Splendid, another place I'd rather not be,' muttered

Cyril.

'Don't let this give you too many ideas, Cyril,' said Lawrence. 'But we have our swords with us this time.'

Cyril smiled, slightly too menacingly for Lawrence's liking, before catching sight of something strange.

'Wait, what's going on there?' said Cyril.

Lawrence turned to see E.V. hand-feeding meat to one of the microdraconyx.

'Oh no, that is not right at all,' said Lawrence. 'And I thought snake-charming was insane.'

'We should probably go over and supervise her,' suggested Cyril.

They climbed down from their horses and walked them up to where E.V. was kneeling. She looked up, smiling when she saw them.

'Hello, Your Highness, Mr Toadstool.'

'E.V., do you realise what you're doing?' asked Lawrence.

'Feeding a dragon,' E.V. shrugged. 'Any objections?'

'It's a bad idea,' said Cyril.

A little way back, on the edge of the forest, he noticed the other two dragons were also feeding on meat, which E.V. had clearly given them.

'Not for somebody who knows how to tame them,' she replied. 'These dragons don't usually come out this early. I wonder what happened.'

'We can answer that,' said Lawrence.

They told E.V. about the roar of the fire-breathing dragon.

'Ah, so that's what it was.' E.V. stood between them,

put her arms around their shoulders and turned them away from the dragons as she continued. 'Why would a dragon make such a sudden gesture of aggression like that?'

The three dragons were secretly listening.

'Well, we didn't mean to,' said Lawrence. 'But we were there, and by chance we angered the beast.'

There was a growl from behind.

'Cyril, onto the horses!' yelled Lawrence.

But it was too late: the dragons pounced and Cyril and Lawrence pulled out their swords again. The crested dragon pinned Cyril down on his back, but Finnegan swiftly galloped to his rescue, kicking the dragon with his hind legs. They went on fighting until two of the dragons fell off the edge of the hill and down into the ravine. The last dragon, the hooked-clawed dragon, reared upright in front of Cyril and was about to slash him, when it was distracted by the smell of the snake repellent. It hesitated, giving Cyril just enough time to impale his sword through its body as it pinned him down again. The dragon dragged a claw down Cyril's head before collapsing to the ground, and Cyril pulled out his sword, leaving the dragon's body to drop over the edge.

'Oh, gosh!' E.V. rushed over and knelt down between Cyril and Lawrence. 'Are you alright?'

Just before they sat up, E.V. slipped two small, disc-like objects into their coat pockets.

'Oh,' said Cyril. 'What happened?'

'I don't think they'll be bothering us again,' said Lawrence.

'You were both brave to fight those dragons,' said E.V.

'Please, enough about fighting dragons!' said Cyril as he stood up. 'My father has a long story to tell when I arrive home.'

'Yes, it is getting quite late,' said Lawrence. 'Do you think you could go back home by yourself, Cyril? It's only a short walk away.'

'Of course,' said Cyril.

'Have a safe ride back, then.'

They put their swords away, but didn't say goodbye to E.V. They simply turned their backs on her and walked away, without so much as a backward glance.

Meanwhile, back at Cyril's tree, the candelabras in the dining room were being lit and the toadstools outside were beginning to glow. The Queen was sitting at the dining room table, looking worried as the King put his cloak on.

'Do you think you should take a few soldiers with you?' asked the Queen.

'It's getting dark now,' said the King. 'What's the worst that can happen? I won't come back until I've found him. I promise.'

Just then, Cyril came bursting through the door from the stable, looking exhausted and terrified. The Queen stood up instantly and rushed towards him.

'Cyril! Thank goodness!' she cried, hugging him tightly. 'I'm so glad you're safe. Where's Lawrence?'

'He asked me to make my own way home as it was getting so late,' Cyril explained.

'Oh, Cyril,' said the Queen, with her arms around him. She looked down at Cyril's ruined coat and trousers. 'What happened to your clothes? Don't tell me you were attacked by dragons?'

'Fooled you again, didn't I?' Cyril said wearily. 'I've even got this…' He took the disc out of his pocket that E.V. had given him. It looked like a medal of some kind, and the Queen read it: *'For courage against wild animals*, it says. Now that's very convincing. Oh, you have a cut on your head too…how did you manage that? What really happened Cyril? Come to think of it, I can't imagine Lawrence being in on a joke that would leave you injured like this. Is Finnegan okay?'

'Apart from a battered ankle, yes.'

'A battered…oh, you can tell me about it later, Cyril. I've been so worried about you today.'

'And with good reason…' Cyril presented the folded-up leaf. He sat down at the table, unfolded the leaf and told his parents the whole story.

'So, you were guilty of murder and never told me?' he asked the King sullenly.

'We didn't want you to worry,' the King answered.

'You see, Cyril…' said the Queen. 'You will eventually come to realise that your parents are not perfect.'

'It looks like learning how to run a Kingdom is going to take me longer than I thought,' sighed Cyril.

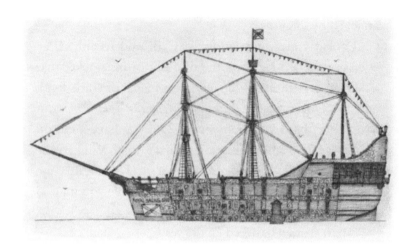

CHAPTER IV
THE ROYAL PARTY

Summer was in full swing, and one warm, sunny morning Cyril, his parents, his uncle Prince Matthias and all of their horses, including their spare horse Elizabeth, were standing together by the front gates of Cyril's tree. It was the day of the Royal Party, for which they were all dressed in their most formal attire, though Cyril's parents were not wearing their crowns. The Queen wore white gloves, with a dark cloak over her dress, and Cyril, Matthias and the King wore dark blue coats, without epaulettes, and black ribbons around their collars. Cyril also wore the medal E.V. had given him, sewn onto his coat.

'Cyril, when was the last time you went out with us?' asked the Queen.

Cyril thought for a moment.

'It couldn't have been when that autumn thunderstorm flooded the tree, could it?' suggested the King.

'Not counting last year's Royal Party, I think it might have been,' said Cyril.

'It's the same year after year,' said Matthias. 'But I have a feeling that today will be different.'

'I think you may be right.' The Queen put her hand on Cyril's shoulder.

'Are we going to get a move on then?' asked Cyril.

'Yes, we are,' said the Queen.

They made their way out of the gates and climbed onto their horses, before riding out into the countryside. It was a bright, dry day, the ideal weather for such an occasion.

The Royal Sailing Ship was moored at the harbour, waiting for them. She had received a new coat of purple paint, and lots of little flags had been attached along the overhead centre rope, from the bow mast to the stern. She was a large, majestic vessel compared to the others in the port, broad enough to carry numerous passengers.

On a field of grass by the harbour, friends and relatives of the royal family were all waiting to board the ship. Some of them were people who Cyril had recently met, including Lawrence, Mel, Lydia and even the witches. They had been attending the Royal Party every year for several years now and, as always, they were dressed in their best clothes, though many of them were still wearing their travelling cloaks.

As the royals appeared on the hill opposite the ship, everyone in the field looked up at them and bowed down. The royals bowed their heads in return, holding still for a few seconds.

During this moment of pause, Lydia, her head close to the ground whilst bowing, spotted something in a box next to her. It looked not unlike parsley. Curious, she secretly nabbed some, as the royals dismounted from their horses.

'The horse pen is over there,' said Matthias, pointing to a square of white fencing filled with other horses.

'I do feel sorry for the horses sometimes,' said the Queen. 'Always being left behind. We should make it up to them whenever we can.'

They went over to the pen, ushering the horses inside, while the Queen took a moment to open the satchel around Elizabeth's neck and retrieve her hat.

'In you go, Finnegan,' said Cyril.

Finnegan walked calmly into the pen and Cyril closed the gate behind him, before joining his family as they headed down the hill.

When the royals finally arrived in the field by the harbour, the guests cleared a path for them to walk down, allowing them to make their way up the wooden boarding ramp and onto the ship. Once on the ship, Cyril turned, gesturing to the guests.

'Well? What are you waiting for?' he called to the crowd. 'All aboard!'

While everyone was boarding the ship, the King and

Queen made their way into the dining room, a vast room with a red carpet, a long, mahogany table and lots of varnished chairs.

'This looks quite splendid, as always,' the Queen remarked.

'Let's hope Cyril doesn't interfere with it,' muttered the King.

They walked over to one of the many portholes, lined with turquoise curtains, and gazed at the sea outside.

'Don't worry,' the King reassured his wife. 'Everything will be fine.'

'Cyril has never known what it's like to be the centre of attention at a formal occasion such as this,' said the Queen. 'He has little sense of charm, and I worry about him. At least his vocabulary's improving.'

'Today could be the day his life changes,' said the King. 'He cannot remain immature for much longer than this.'

The Queen took off her cloak and hung it on a nearby stand, revealing her heavy, cream-coloured dress, and she placed her hat on her head.

'To the main deck?' asked the King.

'Yes,' said the Queen. 'I tell you what, why don't we let Cyril steer the ship for a little while?'

'What for?' asked the King.

'You know there's an observation chamber at the bottom of the ship?' said the Queen. 'Well, I reckon there are some beautiful reefs and fish in the tropics. Cyril will almost certainly take his time, trying to find the way to the island. If, and when, he starts to delay us, we can take the opportunity to go down and enjoy the beautiful ocean life.'

'That sounds like a good idea,' said the King. 'But what will we do about lunch?'

'I'll tell Lydia to prepare ours for later. It means we shan't be dining with everyone else this time, but we *will* get to enjoy some rare views of the underwater world.'

'Shall we go and surprise Cyril then?'

Cyril was on the main deck, peering over the edge of the ship at the buildings on the coast.

Lawrence came up onto the deck as well and Cyril turned around to greet him.

'Ah, morning, Lawrence.'

They shook hands. Lawrence was wearing white tights, a frilly shirt and a brown, formal coat.

'How are you feeling about this journey at sea then, Cyril?'

'Well, I know this is supposed to be the day of the party, and I should really be thinking about that. But I distinctly remember there being an observation chamber on the ship that enables you to see the fish underwater as you sail past them and, well, since you're here, if you have the time, I was wondering whether you could help me study the animals in the water?'

'I had a feeling you might ask me that,' Lawrence smiled, pulling out his handbook from his coat pocket. 'So, I came prepared.'

Cyril grinned, looking forward to learning more about the Kingdom's creatures, and he and Lawrence made their way to the front of the main deck. Everyone had been commanded to report to the main deck on arrival and it was filling up fast. Once all the guests were in attendance, the King and Queen appeared on the balcony, behind which was the ship's steering wheel.

'Ladies and gentlemen,' announced the Queen. The guests all looked up at her as she continued. 'Welcome aboard the Royal Sailing Ship. Some of you have never been on this journey before, and I do hope you enjoy the experience. Those who have been before, we thank you for joining us for yet another gathering.'

The King stepped forward. 'For this year's Royal party, we will be sailing to the tropical island of Acrodryohydrus, where the tallest palm trees, on the top of our green world, are surrounded by water. It will take approximately an hour to get there, so please enjoy the sea breeze and the breath-taking views whilst we travel. In five minutes time, the ship will set sail. Luncheon will be served for the Royal family when the second bell is rung upon arrival at our destination.'

The Queen spoke again. 'We want you to know that we, the royal family, put our guests before ourselves on this ship. You are our highest priority. Now, please, enjoy yourselves.'

Shortly, the bell behind the King and Queen rang and the guests cleared the deck. The King and Queen walked over to their son who was still standing on the main deck, looking out to sea.

'Cyril?' said the Queen.

'Yes?' Cyril replied.

'How would you like to steer the ship?' she asked.

Cyril paused, incredulous. 'Are you being serious?'

'As long as you know your way to the island,' said the King.

'You can ask one of the sailors to help you navigate if you need to,' assured the Queen. 'But the ship is otherwise yours.'

'That's amazing! Thank you!' exclaimed Cyril, delighted.

The ship's lieutenant came to report to the royals. His indigo coat and flat, triangular hat were worn by most of the crew as their uniform.

'Majesties? Your Highness?' he said. 'I must ask you to clear the deck so that the crew can man the ropes and unfurl the sails.'

'Of course.' Cyril eagerly climbed up the steps to the steering wheel and nudged the captain out of the way. 'I'll take it from here! This is Prince Cyril, now unfurl those sails!'

The crew swiftly got to work on the ropes and sails, which soon caught the wind. As the harbour workers disconnected the ropes from the quayside, the ship swung around and started to sail alongside the coastline, in a southerly direction. The King and Queen came back to join Cyril.

'You will be careful, won't you, Cyril?' said the Queen. 'This is a necessary skill for you to practice, for when you're a King and your people depend on you. But it can be dangerous.'

'Oh, don't worry, Mum. I'll be careful,' assured Cyril.

'There can be nasty killers in these waters,' warned the

King.

'I know,' said Cyril.

A little later, as they travelled further south into the open ocean, Mel Blue-Bottom wandered into the ship's vast lounge area to find Vincent Verccito sitting at a table by one of the windows. The artist had a pencil and a pad of paper in hand and was busy capturing the view.

'Good day, Mr Verccito,' Mel said. 'Mind if I sit down?'

'Morning, Mr Blue-Bottom. Please do.'

Mel took the seat opposite. 'What are you sketching there?'

'Merely a view of the land from the sea. I have been meaning to ask, how would you feel about the possibility of my illustrations featuring in your books?'

'Well, you are a fine artist, I must say, if a little too imaginative.'

'But imagination is vital,' declared Vincent. 'Don't you write fiction books?'

'I have written some, but most people, when reading them, would prefer to use their own imaginations rather than look upon illustrations.'

'Perhaps…shall we have a drink?' asked Vincent, looking a little uncertain.

'Very well,' said Mel.

They walked over to the bar in the lounge and ordered two small glasses of whisky.

'Have you met up with the young Prince lately?' asked Vincent, while they waited to be served.

'I have indeed,' Mel replied. 'He came to ask me about

the coastal primates.'

Their drinks were served, and they both took a few sips.

'Those coastal primates you speak of are very savage, aren't they?' said Vincent. 'It makes one wonder who, or what, created them.'

They continued talking and drinking, and Mel eventually looked a little tipsy from the whisky. 'As I was telling the Prince not so long ago, they appear to share many common traits with us civilised folk. For instance, they have opposable thumbs, and their bone structure is not so different to our own. It is almost certain that we are related to them in some way.'

'I'm not sure I like this attitude, Melvyn,' remarked Vincent. 'I knew I shouldn't have asked you to have a drink with me—'

'I am not drunk!' protested Mel. 'It's true. We share a good many of their features.'

The ridges on Vincent's earflaps turned red.

'Your ears…' said Mel. 'They're flushing with blood…'

'It happens whenever I'm stressed.' Vincent spoke with a clipped tone, growing increasingly frustrated with Mel and his bizarre ideas.

'Do you eat meat?' asked Mel.

'Of course!' Vincent exclaimed. 'For goodness' sake, why?'

'Perhaps you are a missing link between the two species of coastal primate…'

Vincent stood up. 'I've had quite enough of this nonsense. Good day.'

He stormed off, back to his table, as Mel stood for a moment, deep in thought, before heading upstairs towards the main deck.

Lydia was making herself at home in the galley kitchen, having already hung her cloak and blue hat on the hook by the door. Her dress, like her hat, was blue, as were her gloves, which she had removed and placed on the side. She also wore a pair of opal earrings and a purple bow with ribbons around her neck.

While she was inspecting the galley, the three witches came in, all wearing more formal versions of their usual long, black dresses. They took off their tall, black hats as they entered.

'Morning, ladies,' said Lydia. 'Another party, another feast.'

'Will we be cooking the same as usual?' asked the pink-eyed witch.

'Yes, the same as always, though I think there are more vegetarians on this occasion.'

There was a knock at the door and Lydia opened it to find Cyril standing there. 'Oh, morning, Your Highness.'

'L…Lydia!' he stuttered. 'Why, I didn't know you were on board!'

Lydia smiled warmly. 'Is there something I can help you with?' she asked.

'I was just wondering whether you could delay my lunch by half an hour,' said Cyril.

'Yes, I am sure I can do that, Your Highness.'

'Please, call me Cyril.'

'As you wish, Cyril. May I ask, why the lunch postponement?'

'I'm…I'm going down to the bottom of the ship. There's a chamber down there with giant portholes, through which you can see all the fish as they swim past the ship.'

'Well, I hope you find some interesting animals down there. There could be all sorts of creatures underneath us.'

'Yes, well…if you could please start cooking everyone else's food about half-an-hour earlier than normal, and then prepare mine for when we reach the island,' said Cyril. 'It will be a nice surprise for everyone to enjoy their lunch whilst still on the journey.'

'No problem. I'll have the bell rung as well.'

'Perfect. I'll see you later then,' said Cyril. 'Oh, one other thing. Please, don't tell my parents about this change of plan.'

'As you wish,' said Lydia.

Cyril smiled, patting her awkwardly on the shoulder as he left the galley.

The witches were preparing wood to put underneath the galley's three cauldrons, chopping food and looking up recipes.

'I suppose I shall have to lay the table,' Lydia sighed, taking a white tablecloth out of a cupboard and heading through to the dining room.

The ship was sailing through warm, turquoise water as they approached Acrodryohydrus, and the islands lush rainforest and vibrant underwater coral reef were just about visible from the deck of the ship. Suddenly, to the surprise of most of the passengers, the sails were lifted, and the lunch bell rang as the ship came to a stop.

The King and Queen were in the lounge and could just about see the island through one of the portholes.

'Ah, we're slowing down a bit short of our destination,' said the Queen. 'Cyril must be struggling and has finally fallen behind schedule.'

'Shall I go and tell them to make us a later lunch?' asked the King.

'No need, I've already seen to that. Now, let us make our way down to this observation chamber.'

The witches were busy stirring the cauldrons and adding garnishes to the passengers' lunch, when Lydia came into the dining room where the other royals were gathering. She called for silence.

'Ladies and gentlemen, I regret to inform you that their Majesties, the King and Queen, and His Royal Highness, Prince Cyril, will not be dining with you all at this time. They have decided to eat later, in order to attend to…other matters.'

The party guests, including Matthias, sat down and resumed their chatter, confused and disappointed at the sudden turn of events.

Cyril and Lawrence were down in the observation chamber, several decks below. The room had a few benches and a massive sheet of viewing glass on each side of the hull, through which they could see lots of different types of fish, swimming around the corals.

'There are more fish than you could ever have imagined, Cyril,' said Lawrence.

'What's that in the distance?' Cyril pointed to a dark shape, swimming through the water.

'That's a plesiosaur. Remember the flying pterosaurs? Well, while they rule the sky, plesiosaurs live in the sea, as do the sea dragons.'

'How can these animals be related to some of the animals we see on land?'

'You recall that I mentioned missing links?' Lawrence turned to a page in his book. 'A missing link between the dragons on land and those in the water is Ichthyodracosaurus. Normally, these creatures live in the rivers near fire-breathing dragon territory. As small dragons took to the water, their descendants' legs became fins, and they developed skin-like membranes, similar to wings.'

'Some of these fish look bigger than the others, and they have arms instead of fins...'

'Those would be the mer-people,' said Lawrence. 'They're like the ichthyodracosaurus, only they're a relative of mammals. You can see their top half is like that of a primate, but their bottom half is like that of a fish. Those thalassopithecus we saw on the beach are the missing link between primates and mer-people.'

'That makes sense,' said Cyril. 'Just how big can animals grow in the sea?'

At that moment, the door opened, and the King and Queen walked inside.

'Mum? Dad?' Cyril turned round. 'What are you doing

here?'

'We were about to ask you the same question, Cyril,' said the King.

'Lawrence agreed to show me the sea life,' said Cyril.

'Wouldn't you like to see the colourful coral reefs from the main deck?' said the Queen.

'Not now. You made me captain of this ship, didn't you? That means I can, though responsibly, make my own decisions. Now, why don't you go and have your lunch?'

'If only we could,' sighed the Queen.

She and the King suddenly turned to look at the opposite pane of glass, and immediately left the room.

'Maybe you can come back down here when we reach the island,' said Cyril.

'Cyril?' said Lawrence. 'I think I know why your parents left just now...'

Cyril turned round and saw a giant monster with a snake-like body, horns and razor-sharp teeth staring at them through the other pane of glass. He was so shocked that he fell over, and in response to his sudden movement, the monster bumped its head on the ship, causing the dinner table above to jiggle. This surprised the guests but there was no apparent danger.

'It's a real sea dragon,' said Lawrence in awe.

'Shall we go up onto the main deck and watch it from above?' Cyril suggested, not wanting to admit that the proximity of the creature made him somewhat nervous.

Lawrence nodded, and they headed back up to the main deck.

The Royal Sailing Ship finally arrived at Acrodryohydrus Island and a wooden ramp was placed in front of the side door, allowing passengers to make their way to and from the ship. There was a beach on the island, gift-and-trinket shops and all kinds of marvellous attractions.

While the guests began to roam the island, Cyril and his parents were having their lunch together in the ship's dining room. The King and Queen did not look overly pleased.

'Don't be sad,' said Cyril. 'I got us here safely, didn't I? And you got the chance to eat with me.'

Lydia came out of the galley with something green in her hands. 'Majesties? Your Highness? I was wondering if perhaps you would care to try some of this parsley with your luncheon. I had been planning to give it to you earlier, but it slipped my mind.'

'Oh yes please. I would very much like to try it,' said Cyril, as Lydia came towards him.

She held the parsley above Cyril's head, like mistletoe, and they looked deep into each other's eyes. Cyril thought Lydia was a beautiful creature. But their moment was broken as she lowered the parsley into his mouth, and Cyril automatically started chewing.

'This is rather nice. Where did you get it, as a matter of interest?'

'Um...' Lydia paused for a moment. 'Some loyal friends gave it to me,'

The witches could see and hear what was happening through the windows of the galley doors.

'So that's where it went!' said the tailed witch.

'Why don't we prepare the cauldrons one last time?' said the pink-eyed witch, with a malicious glint in her eye.

The others nodded and the pink-eyed witch opened the door, beckoning Lydia over.

'Please excuse me,' said Lydia, walking back into the galley and closing the doors behind her.

Cyril sat still and quiet for a moment.

'Are you alright, Cyril?' asked the King.

'Yes, I think so,' said Cyril, slowly.

'Well, if you're finished, why don't you go ashore and have a walk along the beach?' advised the Queen.

'I'll do that,' said Cyril, standing up. 'It will clear my head, I'm sure.'

But just as he left the room and headed out into the corridor, Cyril heard a banging and crashing sound coming from the galley. The door leading to the galley was locked. He was about to knock and demand to know what was going on, when he heard a strange scraping noise, coming from the other side. He then caught sight of the key for the door by his feet. Not wanting to get involved, but concerned that something, or someone, might be trapped on the other side, he quietly slipped the key underneath the door, before heading out onto the main deck.

In the galley, Lydia was tied up in the corner by the door, not knowing what to do. But when she saw the key suddenly appear on the floor she reached for it, managing to grab it with her tail. The witches were firing up the cauldrons again, having already barricaded the dining room doors.

'I'm truly sorry that I took your parsley,' said Lydia, desperately. 'It was my animal instinct. Please, give me another chance.'

'Another chance to steal, I suppose,' said the pink-eyed witch.

Lydia tried hard to bend her flexible body and place the key in the lock behind her with her teeth. Once in the locking mechanism, she rattled the key.

The tailed witch caught her. 'Oh no you don't! I'm not letting you slip through my fingers again!'

The witch turned the key in the lock and took the key away. What she did not realise was that she had just unlocked the door, rather than locking it, but that was the way Lydia had planned it. While the witch looked for somewhere to hide the key, Lydia, still tied up, carefully pushed the door open and crawled out into the hallway, slowly inching her way down the corridor and into the dining room.

The King and Queen were still in there, so they were most surprised to see Lydia suddenly appear, tied up on the floor.

'Miss Lydia!' cried the Queen, as she stood up. 'What happened?'

'The witches tied me up, Your Majesty.'

'Those insolent…creatures!' said the King. 'How dare they!'

'Now, now, dear, calm down,' said the Queen.

They walked over to Lydia and bent down to untie her. By now, she was sweating, her hair was out of place and her head-crests were blushing.

'Even now, you look most attractive with that head display,' said the King kindly.

'Thank you, Sir,' said Lydia. 'Ow…' she added, turning to the Queen. 'That's my tail.'

'Oh, I am sorry,' said the Queen.

Lydia was soon free of the rope, but she stayed there for a moment as she thanked the King and Queen for their help.

'May I ask how you ended up like that?' said the Queen.

'I stole some of the witches' parsley, Your Majesty,' said Lydia as she stood up. 'I don't fully intend to steal; I just attempt to borrow without permission. It's an urge, or an instinct, that I've always had and have struggled to overcome. The rest of my family also used to do it, to an extent. I am beginning to wonder whether what Your Majesty's son told me is indeed true.'

'What is that?' asked the King. 'That he loved you from the moment he set eyes on you?'

'No, Your Majesty. Believe it or not, he suggested that I was an animal, that we are all animals.'

'You know, I have been wondering the same thing myself,' said the Queen. 'We have seen the coastal primates and their resemblance to ourselves, not to mention that we have made our home out of a tree.'

'That doesn't mean a great deal,' said the King.

'And crests and a tail do, Your Majesty?' asked Lydia, pointedly.

'I never mentioned that,' said the King.

'No, but…never mind. I really must insist you let me

escape, before the witches come looking for me,' said Lydia.

'Of course,' said the Queen. 'You may be excused. We will have a strong word with the witches for you.'

'Thank you, Majesties.'

Lydia left the dining room, cautiously looked both ways and ran out onto the main deck.

'I think we could do with some fresh, tropical air after all that, don't you?' said the Queen.

'I could do with a pint at the bar,' said the King. 'But we had best speak to the witches first and find that son of ours.'

Out on the deck, leaning against the edge of the ship, looking out to sea, was E.V. She was smartly clothed in a pink dress and hat, but she still looked mischievous.

'Nobody needs saving then?' she said to no-one in particular. 'Goodness, why does nothing interesting happen around here?'

Cyril appeared at the edge of the ship alongside her. 'Oh, it does.'

'Your Highness? You found my medal I see.' E.V. had caught sight of the decoration on Cyril's coat.

'You said you wanted to see something interesting?' said Cyril. 'Have you ever wondered what might be down there in the water, in this part of the world?'

'Yes, but I've never known how to find out,' said E.V., eagerly.

Cyril's chance to get his own back on E.V. had come. He grabbed hold of her and vaulted her over the side, watching gleefully as she hit the water with a loud splash.

Cyril pretended to be horrified. 'Oh, gracious! The horror! I need assistance!'

Just then, his parents appeared.

'What's happening now?' asked the Queen.

'Emilia here has taken a tumble into the water,' said Cyril.

He saw a rope in the Queen's hands, the one that the witches had used to restrain Lydia, and grabbed it, throwing one end over the side. He yelled to E.V.

'Grab the rope!'

'I don't like the look of this at all,' said the Queen.

But, barely a second later, there was a tug on the other end of the rope and Cyril pulled with all his might. His parents instantly took hold of the rope too and they gently pulled E.V. back onto the deck. She seemed unconscious and there was a crab clinging onto her dress.

'Oh no you don't,' said Cyril. 'Ouch!'

His parents were shocked as he picked up the crab and threw it back overboard.

'Right, let's fill this casualty with air.' Cyril knelt next to E.V., pressing down on her body several times, until he realised that she was on her front. He turned her over.

'A few slaps to the face should do the trick…'

After a few slaps, E.V. eventually coughed and sat up.

'What the…? Where am I? I rose to the light. Am I…?'

'No, I assure you, you're still with us, E.V.,' said Cyril.

'I feel so weak and dizzy.' E.V. put her hand on her head. 'Where's my hat?'

'Oh, don't worry. I'll fetch it for you.'

Cyril took off his coat and dived off the ship into the water. The water was clear from the surface, but once underneath it, Cyril's eyesight was not. He saw a blurry pink circular object and swam down to pick it up. It was moving, as if it were walking. Once he got hold of it, he came back up for air. The rope was lowered, suggesting his parents were still on the deck above, so he gave the rope a tug, signalling to the King and Queen to hoist him back up. He climbed over the edge when he got to the top and put his feet on the deck, where E.V. was still sitting down.

'Is this it, E.V.?'

'Yes, it is! Thank you!'

Cyril handed the hat to E.V., only to hear her scream in surprise as she discovered another crab, larger this time, sitting inside her hat. She threw it to the side in disgust, but the crab was still clinging to her hat, so the hat went with it. The crab, wearing E.V.'s pink hat, proceeded to scuttle around the deck for a while, before climbing onto a cannon on the other side of the deck and plummeting to the jetty below. E.V. pushed herself upright, made her way down to the side door, down the wooden ramp and onto the white, sandy beach. She soon spotted the hat-stealing crab, weaving its way in between the tables where some of the guests were sitting and she immediately began to chase it.

From the deck, Cyril watched the chaos before him, a manic grin on his face. 'Yes, I finally got my own back. You will think twice before messing with this Prince again, lady!'

The King and Queen looked at their son, ashamed. E.V. had chased the crab over to some coconut trees, one of which the crab had crawled up and she was now throwing coconuts at it, in an attempt to make it drop her hat. In the end, the crab became fed up with dodging coconuts and dropped the hat, right into E.V.'s hands. She began to make her way back to the ship, leaving the crab to crawl down from the tree and retreat back into the water.

The Queen placed her hand on Cyril's shoulder. 'Revenge won't solve anything, Cyril,' she said softly.

'Why not?' asked Cyril. 'She knows how I feel now; we're even.'

'That's just the point,' said the Queen. 'Now, *you're* just as bad as *she* is. What did she even do to you to make you behave this way?'

'She's always bragging about her safety and survival skills, and then she catches you by surprise with a demonstration, which always fails. I'm telling you, she's crazy; she doesn't deserve to be at this party.'

The Queen turned to the King and they spoke quietly to one another.

'There is madness everywhere, it seems,' sighed the King.

'I just hope Emilia has learned her lesson,' muttered the Queen. 'So that our errant son doesn't decide to teach her another.'

By mid-afternoon, the sails were unfurled, and the Royal Sailing Ship began its journey back to the mainland.

The King and Queen were down in the observation chamber, admiring the Acrodryohydrus reef as they passed it. The colourful coral was a wonder to behold, as were the tropical fish which darted in and out of the coral structures. Cyril had dried himself off after his great hat-rescue attempt and had decided to wander down into the ship's ballroom. He could hear the music of the string quartet before he entered the room and the soft sound of multiple dancing footsteps. As he walked through the grand white doors, the people nearest the entrance bowed down to him.

'It's quite alright, no need for that,' said Cyril. 'I'm really not sure I deserve such respect.'

He quickly spotted Lydia, who was lingering near one of the portholes, and walked towards her.

'Afternoon, Lydia. Are you here to dance or to enjoy the food?'

'Well, I am grazing at the moment, Cyril,' said Lydia. 'But I was hoping to dance eventually. Do you know how to dance?'

'I think I remember a little.'

'Shall we then?' Lydia suggested, holding out her right hand.

Cyril paused for a few seconds before bowing and taking Lydia's offered hand. Lydia smiled, taking hold of her dress with her left hand and Cyril's waist with her tail, as they drifted towards the dancefloor and began dancing. Other guests began to dance around them as the music continued. It took only a moment for Lydia's crests to take on a rose-pink hue.

'How do you feel, Cyril?' she asked.

'I feel like I'm in a different world,' smiled Cyril, gazing at her. '…without any troubles.'

They wobbled slightly, drawing closer together, as the ship was swayed by the waves.

'I know it's a little more difficult to get the steps right, but I think the way the ship moves encourages you to dance,' said Lydia.

'Yes, usually, this ballroom is used when the ship is moored in foreign harbours,' said Cyril. 'It provides accommodation for when we socialize with our friends or relatives.'

Lydia nodded and they continued to dance until the music ended. As they came to a stop, they rested their foreheads against one another.

'That was lovely, Cyril,' said Lydia. 'You certainly are energetic.'

'You're something of a natural dancer yourself,' said Cyril.

'A natural?' said Lydia. 'Well, for a time I did—'

'But yes, I am energetic, am I not?' interrupted Cyril. 'I've got to be strong, brave and heroic, the makings of a true prince.'

'Ah, yes, I've been meaning to ask…' said Lydia, slightly changing the subject. 'What does that decoration on your coat say?'

'Oh, E.V. gave me that for fighting alligators and dragons.'

Cyril held on to Lydia's arm as they began to stroll around the edge of the ballroom.

'You know, as strange as it may seem to some, I think you may be right about our place in nature,' said Lydia.

'Oh, yes,' said Cyril. 'We're all on the same family tree.'

Lydia took a deep breath and stood with her back to the wall. 'It's made me realise…I really don't think I'm the right species to…I don't think it's right for me to spend too much time with a prince or the royal family of a different…animal type.'

'You're not *that* different, Lydia,' said Cyril. 'You're like me, in many ways.'

'That's what I'm afraid of. Could you please excuse me?' Lydia turned to go but Cyril held her back.

'You can't walk out on the Prince,' commanded Cyril.

'Cyril,' said Lydia, firmly, but with a hint of sadness in her eyes. 'I'm too old for you and we're too alike. I don't want your feelings to get any stronger. You're still so young.'

Cyril hesitated as Lydia gave him a kiss on the cheek.

'Farewell, darling.' She turned away from Cyril and walked gracefully and quickly from the ballroom, to the surprise of the other guests.

Cyril watched her go, a terrible ache growing inside him. His cousins, Mary and Fergus, noticed his distress and came over to comfort him.

'Don't you worry, Cyril,' said Mary. 'She might not be the one to fall in love with, but I'm sure she will still be a good friend to you.'

'*I've* never fallen in love,' said Fergus. 'Romance is not all that dependable.'

Cyril, though, was too depressed to take them

seriously.

The ship arrived back at the dock just as the sun was setting, and the passengers made their way down the ramp, setting off to collect their horses or make their way home on foot.

The Queen found Cyril sitting on a musician's chair in the ballroom, with his back to her. His head was bowed.

'Cyril?' she said, walking over to him.

'Oh, hello, Mum,' Cyril murmured.

'We're back at the dock now,' said the Queen. 'Shall we go and fetch the horses?'

'I don't feel well,' said Cyril quietly, turning round with a melancholy look. 'I think…I think I might be…in love.'

The Queen knew how he was feeling, and this looked serious.

Cyril was glad to be off the ship and back in the safety of his bedroom again. He was dressed in his night gown, sitting on his bed with the Queen's arm around him.

'I'm so sorry you feel like this, Cyril,' the Queen sympathized.

'References to love in a romantic sense always used to make me feel sick,' sighed Cyril. 'But never in this way.'

'This emotion is just a part of growing up,' continued the Queen. 'Get some sleep, dear. You've had a busy day.'

Cyril hugged his toy unicorn and the Queen gently lay his quilt over him. Nancy was sitting in a chair next to the bed.

'Please, put his mind at rest, Nancy,' said the Queen.

'Yes, Ma'am,' said Nancy.

'Goodnight, Mum,' said Cyril.

'Goodnight, Cyril,' said the Queen, closing the door behind her.

'Now, Your Highness,' said Nancy. 'Which story would you like me to read to you?'

The Queen was walking down the stairs with the King and Matthias.

'So, Cyril's experiencing love-sickness at last?' said Matthias.

'Yes, he is,' said the Queen. 'I do hope it doesn't last too long. He's so close to full maturity now.'

'It has to be said, though,' said the King. 'Lydia is some animal, charming and handsome in many ways.'

'Well, I wish the best for Cyril,' said Matthias. 'Tell him he is welcome to come to my home at any time.'

'Thank you, Matthias,' said the Queen, kissing him on the cheek.

CHAPTER V

THE RELIABLE CARER

Cyril had been very emotional since the last Royal Party; he was reaching full maturity and the feeling of this transformation was clearly affecting him. But, after a few weeks, he was finally able to take his mind off the situation, and so the Queen sent a pigeon to Lawrence's laboratory, asking him when he was next available.

The following week, Lawrence arrived at the King and Queen's home, and Cyril came into the dining room to find his parents sitting with Lawrence at the table.

'Where are we going this time then?' asked Cyril.

'We're going on a journey across the sea on flying horses,' said Lawrence. 'We'll be visiting different islands and studying their environments. You'd best bring those swords again, and dress very warmly.'

While Cyril went to fetch his coat and the swords, the King and Queen took Lawrence out into the passageway and spoke to him.

'I don't blame you, Mr Toadstool,' said the Queen. 'But I was most worried the last time you took Cyril out.'

'To tell you the truth, Ma'am, so was I,' admitted Lawrence.

'We've been going insane worrying about the entire ordeal,' said the King. 'But his life must progress somehow.'

'Even though we do not wish to send him out there, we must. So here, you can have this.' The Queen handed him a wad of money. 'For twice your usual pay, please do everything in your power to protect Cyril from danger.'

'Well, thank you, Your Majesty,' said Lawrence.

'Just don't tell Cyril about it,' added the Queen.

Cyril came back downstairs with the swords, dressed in his warm clothes.

'Remember, Cyril,' said the Queen. 'Be very careful, and don't cause any trouble.'

'Yes, Mum.'

Later that morning, Cyril and Lawrence arrived at the Flying-Horse-for-Hire stable. The black, wooden stable sat in the middle of a field of grass, with the sea visible on the horizon. A large brass medallion, with the image of a flying horse on it, was affixed above the stable doors.

'This is where you come if you want to fly,' said Lawrence.

'Have you done this before?' asked Cyril.

'Oh, yes,' said Lawrence. 'I've flown to nearly all the corners of the Kingdom, but this time I'm taking a prince with me.'

They climbed off Finnegan and Sebastian and walked them into the stable. A tiny, friendly-looking man, with pointy ears and orange eyes and wearing sturdy boots and a thick, casual coat, was leaning on one of the horse pens. He looked up as Cyril and Lawrence entered.

'Hello again, Mr Toadstool,' he said jovially. 'Say, is this the young Prince?'

'Yes, it is,' said Lawrence.

'Well, I'm delighted to meet you, Your Highness,' the man said, reaching up and shaking Cyril's hand.

'Obviously,' replied Cyril, haughtily.

The man looked a little taken aback by Cyril's tone, but dutifully removed the saddles and bridles from Finnegan and Sebastian and led them into a pen. A short while later, he came back, leading out two flying horses.

'I've got just the pair of flyers for you,' he said, presenting Cyril and Lawrence with the two graceful steeds, one black and the other white. 'Their names are Gomez and Jabez. You might want to say hello and stroke them first.'

Cyril and Lawrence did so, speaking politely and giving the animals a stroke while the riding gear was fitted. Once everything was ready, they headed out of the stable.

Fortunately, it wasn't too windy, and the sea on the horizon was sparkling.

'Are you sure this gear will keep us safe?' asked Cyril.

'It couldn't be safer,' said Lawrence. 'I've flown lots of times.'

'One other thing, Lawrence…' Cyril took Lawrence round the back of the stable. 'My parents have been going on and on at me ever since you brought me home from the Reptile Kingdom.'

'You know they're only thinking about what's best for you, Cyril. It's because they care about you.'

'I just hope you don't forbid me to do *too* much today,' said Cyril. 'I'm really not supposed to do this, but here…' Cyril handed Lawrence a sizeable sum of money. 'Take this, on the condition that you will agree to take me to whichever island I choose.'

Lawrence did not look very happy, but he nodded and put the money in his pocket.

'Don't tell my parents about it though,' said Cyril. 'Shall we go then?'

'Yes,' sighed Lawrence. 'Oh please, this cannot be happening to me,' he whispered to himself, as they put their warm cloaks on.

When Cyril had climbed onto Gomez and Lawrence onto Jabez, the two horses opened their huge wings. As Cyril and Lawrence turned them towards the sea, they reared up onto their back legs and charged towards the coast, flapping their wings until they were lifted into the air.

'I love this!' said Cyril.

'I was hoping you would!' replied Lawrence.

'What happens if the horses need to land and there is no land?'

'We can float on water, Your Highness,' said Gomez.

'Yes, they're very useful animals,' said Lawrence.

A short flight later, they began to approach what looked like a forest island, coated mostly in trees but with a few cliffs, small open spaces and lakes dotted around, alongside some rather posh-looking houses.

'That's Dryohydrus Island,' said Lawrence. 'It's where we'll make our first stop.'

The horses dipped into a dive, preparing to land on one of the long beaches. They swooped down, close to the sand, and gently lowered their hooves to ensure a soft landing. Gradually, they came to a stop.

'What an achievement!' said Cyril. 'I've flown over the sea!'

Lawrence climbed off Jabez and set foot on the sand. 'Look, Cyril.'

Cyril climbed off Gomez and looked to where Lawrence was pointing. They could just about see another island in the distance.

'That Cyril, is a desert island,' said Lawrence. 'Notice that the water around it is a lighter colour?'

'Yes, and I can see a huge beam of light,' said Cyril.

'It's the sunlight,' said Lawrence. 'The area of the map closest to the path of the sun is the warmest, and the area furthest-away is the coldest, which is why there are ice caps in the South of the Kingdom. The presence and absence of light make a surprisingly big difference to the temperature, you know.'

'What are we going to do for the time being?' asked Cyril.

'We'll walk through this forest and see what animals we can find.'

They started to hike through the forest, with their flyers following behind. The horses had folded their wings, to make travelling through the dense woodland easier. The trees were tall and brimming with leaves, making the forest dark and gloomy in places, but some light made it down to the forest floor, enabling small flowers to grow.

'We've been going through these trees for a while now,' said Cyril. 'I don't see any animals.'

'Look up into the trees,' said Lawrence.

Cyril looked up and spotted some small birds and squirrels, flitting through the canopy. 'Why aren't there any animals on the ground?'

'I was just wondering the same thing myself,' said Lawrence.

They heard a low, threatening growl and Lawrence took out his sword. 'Predators. Being in a forest is never without risk.'

Cyril took out his sword too. They crept in and out of the trees and soon came to a stream, finding a dead deer lying in the water. Cyril knelt beside it.

'Oh, that is unfortunate, Cyril,' said Lawrence.

'Especially for such a proud and gorgeous creature,' said Cyril sadly.

'I know,' said Lawrence. 'These deer are usually

incredibly fast, fast enough to escape from them.'

'Escape from what?'

They heard the roar again.

'Foxes are quite harmless, but wolves are the ones to watch out for,' Lawrence went on. 'We should get back onto the horses.'

They scrambled over to the horses and climbed onto them, with their swords still in hand. A pack of wolves suddenly appeared in front of them, snarling ferociously, but they did not seem to want to attack Cyril and Lawrence while they were on Gomez and Jabez.

'It was you!' yelled Cyril, holding up his sword. 'You're the ones who killed that deer!'

The wolves closed in around them.

'Don't be like that, Cyril,' said Lawrence. 'Otherwise, what happened to that deer is going to happen to us. Come on, boys…'

They made a dash for it and the wolves began to chase them from behind. Cyril looked back, raised his sword and stabbed the nearest wolf in the side of its body.

'Cyril, please be careful!' said Lawrence.

They both continued trying to scare off the wolves with their swords and Cyril even managed to kill one, impaling it with his sword as the creature tried to pounce over him.

'That's for the deer!' he shouted.

Just a few hundred metres ahead was a cliff edge and Gomez and Jabez instinctively began to gallop faster and faster and opened their wings.

'Oh, no!' shouted Cyril.

'Oh, yes!' replied Lawrence.

'You're going for a ride, Your Highness!' laughed Gomez.

Cyril shut his eyes as the horses reached the edge of the cliff and jumped off. This manoeuvre wrong-footed the wolves and a couple of them tumbled off the cliff to the trees below. The horses were diving at first, terrifying Cyril, but they soon levelled out, overshot their due crash point and swooped back up into the sky.

'Are you okay, Cyril?' called Lawrence.

'I'm just glad I haven't had my lunch yet!' answered Cyril. 'I would have lost it.'

'Well, let's put this little stunt behind us and head further south,' said Lawrence.

A little while later, they were flying into cold winds. The sun was bright, but the wings of the horses were beginning to tremble and they could see ice caps below.

'Lawrence...' stuttered Cyril. 'I'm...so...cold! Can...can we...turn back now?'

'We're just going to fly a little further, Cyril,' said Lawrence. 'I want you to see something.'

They came to the edge of the ice caps and hovered above them. Below was what looked like an ice-cold waterfall, disappearing down through the clouds.

'This is the end of the map!' yelled Lawrence above the sound of the wind. 'There are no sea creatures in the water for miles.'

'There are some penguins down there!' said Cyril. 'They're on the ice.'

'Those penguins are the most common animals on these ice caps at the edge of the world,' said Lawrence.

'So, we're now as far away from the sun as possible?' confirmed Cyril.

'Not for much longer!' said Lawrence. 'Come on, let's go and find somewhere warmer!'

Cyril directed Gomez to follow Lawrence and Jabez towards the nearest island. The island was cold and snowy, but there were a few trees scattered around, so it was clearly less hostile than the ice caps. Once they had landed, Cyril and Lawrence managed to find a sheltered old tree trunk to sit on, where they could make a warm fire and eat their lunch.

'Cyril,' said Lawrence. 'It may seem cruel for animals to kill each other like that, but I've told you before, that's nature. Even the centaurs have to feed on meat.'

'Yes, but not primarily,' said Cyril. 'Killing animals for a specialised meat diet just seems evil to me.'

'I know you meant well,' said Lawrence. 'You have to remember that those wolves need to eat other animals to stay alive,' said Lawrence. 'Try to think about how *they* feel.'

'They don't have feelings,' said Cyril. 'They're killers and shouldn't be in this world. I've just had a thought: why did the wolves leave that deer uneaten?'

'Didn't you notice the deer had a leg missing?' said Lawrence. 'And the stream was bloodier than you'd expect one small deer to make it. Also, there was a third antler next to its body.'

'Well, what does the evidence at this gruesome scene

all add up to?' asked Cyril.

'It seems they'd already killed and eaten another deer in the same place, and they probably abandoned the second one and retreated when they heard us approaching.'

'That's cold-blooded carnage,' said Cyril. 'If only we'd have killed those remaining wolves before we left the island.'

Lawrence put his hand on Cyril's shoulder. 'We mustn't cause an extinction. In this case, we mustn't go around killing every wolf until there are no more left, just because they kill other animals. That's the biggest mistake anything in the Animal Kingdom can make.'

'The Animal Kingdom?' said Cyril. 'If only it were *my* Animal Kingdom. Though I suppose it will be, one day, when my parents are no longer around. What is off the edge of the map, by the way? Where does that drop lead to?'

'The pages of time,' said Lawrence. 'Go there, and you'll find yourself in the world of make-believe and childhood memories.'

'Really?' said Cyril.

Just then, Cyril looked out of the forest, and saw a number of white figures moving across an open plain.

'Those are probably snow hares.' Lawrence took out his handbook and turned to a page about the rabbit family. He handed it to Cyril.

'I can barely see them,' said Cyril.

'The very idea,' said Lawrence. 'It's so that predators can't see them. Look, something's chasing after them!'

Cyril stood up and looked closer. He could vaguely see a larger white figure following behind the rabbits.

'That's a smaller cousin of the wolves,' said Lawrence. 'It's called a snow fox.'

'It looks more playful than the wolves,' said Cyril. 'But now I don't feel like finishing my lunch, not at the scene of a hunt like this.'

'Come now, Cyril. Only one body is my concern right now, and your parents...' Lawrence was about to mention the money the Queen gave him, but quickly resisted. 'They really trust me.'

Cyril sighed, closing Lawrence's handbook and he automatically slipped it into his own pocket before he sat back down on the tree trunk and ate the rest of his lunch.

On the wing again, Cyril, Lawrence and the horses were still cold and trembling as they journeyed through icy winds. It had just begun to snow on the previous island, but it was getting warmer as they glided further back into the path of the sun.

'How much longer before we get back?' asked Cyril.

'About twenty minutes,' said Lawrence. 'Don't worry, we'll get back safely.'

Cyril saw the desert island from earlier, down below, in the very centre of the light's path. There were cliffs and rock formations on the island, and herds of magnificent-looking beasts which he couldn't quite make out from this height.

'Ah, that's just the place for me to warm up again!' said Cyril.

'Cyril, stop!'

They stopped and hovered again as Lawrence took Cyril's money out of his pocket and held it out to him.

'You can have your money back. Please don't land there.'

'It's okay, Lawrence,' said Cyril. 'I'm already where I want to be, and you can't stop me now.'

Lawrence watched in horror and disbelief as Cyril swooped down towards the island. Knowing that he could not manage this level of disaster on his own, Lawrence signalled to Jabez, and with great trepidation, they flew swiftly back towards the mainland.

When Cyril landed, he climbed off Gomez and collapsed on the sand, relieved to be warm again.

'Just feel that sunshine on your body. The cold certainly went away quickly, didn't it?'

'Yes, but don't you think we should go back, Your Highness?' asked Gomez.

Cyril was about to respond when he heard some strange noises, coming from somewhere nearby. He stood up and took out his sword, worried that they might encounter another attack.

'I managed to defend myself once, I can defend myself again,' he said to himself.

Both Gomez and Cyril jumped in surprise as a herd of huge, four-legged grey animals appeared, heading towards them. Cyril suddenly remembered that he still had Lawrence's notebook in his pocket, and he quickly took it out, flipping through the pages.

'It's a good thing I put this in my pocket earlier. Oh,

yes, here we are. Those are elephants over there; they shouldn't be a problem.' He turned round and surveyed the rest of the landscape. 'Oh, and those are giraffes over there, and…'

But Cyril stopped, horrified, as he spotted a pride of lions heading towards them. He held up his sword in front of them, while Gomez took on a fiercely protective stance.

'Lions,' said Cyril, quietly. 'I might have known.'

'You dare come here and disturb us?' snarled one of the lions.

'I'm just trying to defend myself,' said Cyril. 'Along with the rest of the Animal Kingdom.'

'This Animal Kingdom is ours,' growled another lion. '…certainly, as far as this island is concerned.'

'Don't you dare come any closer!' said Cyril, stepping back.

There was a whisper from behind, and he and Gomez turned to see a dark-skinned being with a spear, peering over a rocky ledge.

'I recognise you, Your Highness,' the wild man said. 'Come…'

'Go for it, Gomez!' yelled Cyril.

Gomez reared, violently kicking his front legs to keep the lions away, allowing Cyril to jump down over the ridge to safety. But he did not stay there for long. The wild man and his tribe of warriors charged up the ledge to frighten off the lions, and Cyril felt the urge to go up there with them. Like the tribe, he yelled and scrambled back up the ridge, with his sword in hand. He stopped, for it seemed all the lions had been scared off. The tribe roared, and

127

Cyril roared with them, before they bowed down in his honour. Gomez lifted himself off the ledge and lowered himself down towards Cyril, landing in front of him. He was wounded and bleeding slightly.

'Are you alright, Gomez?' asked Cyril.

'Well, I can still fly, can't I?' said Gomez. 'I'll be okay to fly you back, Your Highness. Don't worry.'

There was a village on the other side of the ledge, built just beside some concrete ruins, where the tribe had made their home, and they invited Cyril and Gomez to come and sit with them. As they sat together in a circle, Cyril began to tell the tribe about where he had come from.

'I'm from across the sea,' he told them. 'I soared through the sky on this flying horse.' The tribe turned their attention to Gomez, as Cyril stood up and walked over to him. 'They're the fastest, most magnificent way of travelling.'

'Your Highness?' whispered Gomez. 'Wouldn't you rather be in those old ruins? They look much cooler.'

'No, thanks…' But Cyril suddenly started to feel unwell, and he put his hand to his chest, falling down on his back. The tribe gasped.

'Your Highness!' exclaimed Gomez. 'What's wrong?'

'Something in my body has flared up,' said Cyril weakly.

'Climb onto me, quickly!' said Gomez, sitting down to make it easier for Cyril to climb on him. 'I'll take you back to the mainland.'

Gomez soon appeared in the sky above the Flying-

Horse-for-Hire stable, with the exhausted Cyril on his back. They landed gently, coming to a halt just before the stable doors.

The little owner, who had lent Cyril and Lawrence the flying horses, came out of the stable, confused to find Cyril on the verge of collapse.

'Oh, Your Highness! Is something the matter?'

'I can…barely breathe enough to…speak,' stuttered Cyril.

Finnegan, who was still in the stable, was concerned by Cyril's haggard appearance. 'So, this is what happened to you? I thought Lawrence was in a bit of a hurry.'

'Gomez!' exclaimed the owner. 'What happened to you?'

'I was attacked by some exotic animals, and as…as a matter of fact…I'm beginning to…to feel the same as…the Prince…' Gomez suddenly dropped onto the floor, exhausted.

The owner immediately let Finnegan out of the stable, and Finnegan knelt while the owner helped Cyril onto his back.

'Do you…know your…way home, Finnegan?' murmured Cyril.

'Of course, I do, Cyril,' said Finnegan. 'You just need to hold on. You can rest on my neck if you like.'

Finnegan turned to Gomez and the owner. 'Thank you for your time. I hope Gomez makes a swift recovery.'

'You're welcome, noble one,' said the owner. 'I hope His Highness will be okay too.'

It was raining a while later, but Cyril was safe in bed at home without his quilt over him. The Queen was sitting in a chair next to him, looking concerned, and the King was standing by the door.

'Shall we send a pigeon to the hospital?' the King asked.

'No, he's alright for now,' said the Queen as she stood up. 'In the morning, I will go to the city and find a doctor to examine him.'

'Mum...' said Cyril.

'Yes, sweetheart?' said the Queen, taking her son's hand.

'Lawrence's...book.' Cyril pointed to his coat. 'In...my coat pocket.'

The Queen fumbled inside the pockets of the coat and pulled out Lawrence's handbook.

'What is that doing there?' asked the King.

'Please don't talk to him anymore,' said the Queen. 'He needs to rest. Now, tomorrow, I shall return this to Lawrence, I'll get the money back, and we'll have nothing more to do with the man.'

'M...Money?' murmured Cyril. 'How...how did you...find out?'

The King and Queen looked at each other, confused.

'I think there's more to this situation than we realise,' said the King.

The next morning, after the rain had stopped, the Queen, dressed in a shawl and gloves, set off in a cart pulled by her horse, Gillian, to fetch a doctor and to return

Lawrence's book. They decided to go to Lawrence's laboratory first, but when they got there, the Queen found the building gated and locked, with bars on every window.

'This is Lawrence's laboratory, isn't it?' she said as she climbed down from the cart.

Nervously, she reached through the metal gate and knocked on Lawrence's wooden door. The door opened slowly, to reveal a terrified looking Lawrence.

'Oh, Your Majesty,' he said, bowing to the Queen mournfully.

'Before I give this book back to you, Mr Toadstool…' said the Queen, holding out his book in her hand. '…I will give you two minutes to explain what happened.'

Lawrence rapidly explained the whole story, including the part about Cyril's money, and how overexcited the young Prince had been.

'I see. Well, you had better still have all our money, for your own sake,' said the Queen sternly.

Lawrence gave her a few notes and coins.

'What's this? Where's the rest of it?'

'I spent it on these jail bars, Your Majesty. Here, you can take the keys.' Lawrence held out a ring with keys on it.

'Very well, I think this will suit you best for the time being,' said the Queen. 'Believe me, I do feel sorry for you, but I don't think you should take Cyril on any more expeditions.'

'I understand, Ma'am,' said Lawrence, as she took the keys and handed him back his book.

'I do hope he recovers soon,' added Lawrence.

'Thank you,' said the Queen.

Without another word, she climbed back into the cart and guided Gillian from Lawrence's home. Then they began their journey to the city.

Cyril was awake and resting against the back of the bed by the time the Queen arrived back home.

'Well, Cyril,' said the Queen. 'Lawrence told me what you were up to when he took you on that flight.'

'The money?' said Cyril.

'Yes,' said the Queen.

'I admit it,' said Cyril. 'It was a bad idea. But how did you know about it, last night? You're the one who mentioned the money.'

'Oh…well…I was referring to our own money, which we gave him in exchange for taking care of you,' confessed the Queen.

'I don't understand either of you,' said Cyril, as the Queen sat down on his bed.

'Well, we've got a doctor for you,' she said. 'She's just outside the room.'

'She?'

'You can come in now, Miss Varnish,' said the Queen.

To Cyril's horror, E.V. appeared in the doorway. 'No!' he exclaimed, as he tried to scramble out of bed. But he was still too weak and promptly fell out.

'It's okay, Your Highness,' said E.V. 'All I've ever wanted is a real emergency to deal with.'

She helped the Queen lift Cyril back into bed, where E.V. examined him with the tools from a wooden case she had brought with her. All the while, they explained to her what had happened.

'What's the damage then?' asked the Queen.

'It's a bipolar temperature infection, Ma'am,' explained E.V. 'He was very cold, and then landing on that warm island changed his temperature from very cold to very hot too quickly. It was too much of a shock for his system. Also, with all due respect, those with fair skin and hair seem particularly vulnerable to the heat. He would have been okay if he'd warmed up gradually. He should recover in a few days.'

'Then he'll be well again just in time to attend the opera,' said the Queen.

'Oh, really?' said E.V.

'Yes,' said the Queen. 'For a long time now, we've gone without Cyril. But this year, we finally persuaded him to come.'

'I don't want to keep hearing you say that when we're there,' muttered Cyril.

'I shouldn't worry right now, Your Highness,' said E.V. 'For the moment, you need plenty of rest and lots of nourishing food.' She smiled and then spoke to the Queen. 'I hope you enjoy the opera. I understand that this one is going to be quite different.'

'Thank you, Miss Varnish,' said the Queen. 'You're quite correct, and you've put my mind at ease.'

'You're welcome, Your Majesty,' said E.V.

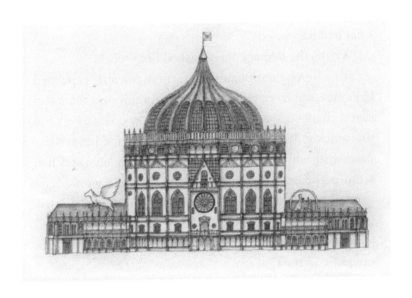

CHAPTER VI

CHANGING NATURE

Cyril had made a full recovery, emotionally and physically, just in time for the King and Queen to take him to the opera. He was in his parents' bedroom where they were all preparing for the evening, donning their grandest outfits. The King and Cyril took less time to get ready than the Queen and were already wearing their long, dark-blue jackets, with black ribbons around their necks. The Queen meanwhile was sitting at her dressing table nearby, having her hair fixed by Nancy.

'Remember, Cyril,' said the King. 'Be sure to make a good impression.'

'Yes, I shall,' said Cyril. 'I'm actually rather looking forward to it.'

The Queen stood up in front of her mirror, admiring her shimmering dark purple dress, complete with a blue satin sash and diamond jewellery. She turned to Cyril and placed her hands on his cheeks.

'Cyril, you'll make a marvellous Prince Charming one day. Oh, I almost forgot...' She opened a small wooden case on her dressing table, inside which sat a silver tiara. 'It has been in the family for years,' she smiled, taking it out of its case and placing it in her dark hair.

'It goes rather well with your complexion, Mum,' said Cyril.

'Thank you, dear,' said the Queen.

'I have to keep remembering that nothing on our bodies is primarily for decoration,' said Cyril.

'Are you wearing your ring as well?' asked the Queen.

'Yes, I thought now would be a good time to wear it,' said Cyril.

'It's 'The Prince's Ring' and is recognised across the Kingdom, you know,' said the Queen.

'Come along, we should be on our way,' said the King.

'Coming, coming,' said the Queen, putting on her white gloves and picking up her fan.

The royal family had a beautiful varnished black carriage, with decorative brass around the outer frame which they used almost exclusively for evenings out. It was waiting at the bottom of the hill just before the gates, with Trevor and Gillian ready to haul it.

Cyril stopped as the carriage door was opened. 'One

last thought. How did you manage to talk me into coming tonight? I want to be sure that I had a good reason for agreeing to this.'

'We'll explain on the way,' said the Queen. 'The light's fading and we ought to get there before the night sets in.'

They climbed into the carriage and, when the door was closed, the gates were opened and Trevor and Gillian pulled the carriage away. From the main doors, Nancy and Reginald watched them leave.

'Well,' said Nancy. 'We've been given the night off. I was thinking I might go for a hike along the cliffs, though I've felt a little uneasy ever since they told me what was special about this particular night at the opera.'

'I hope Cyril now knows enough information about nature to understand,' said Reginald. 'Be prepared for another emotional bedtime for him.'

Inside the carriage, the family were having their discussion.

'That's the problem, Cyril,' said the Queen. 'They have no doubt now that the island will smash into the coast.'

'The opera house is right on the edge of the cliff, remember?' said the King. 'A disaster involving that building was always inevitable.'

'How devastating,' said Cyril. 'Is this going to be their last performance, then?'

'Supposedly, yes,' said the Queen. 'They're holding a ceremonial performance; rather than perform a full-length narrative, they are performing iconic extracts from their most famous productions. This special night will mark the predicted fate of the building.'

'Once the chairs are put back on the tables, the theatre will be cleared, evacuated and abandoned to the oncoming disaster,' said the King.

'Where will their operas be performed from then on?' asked Cyril.

'Right now, they're considering the Beanstalk Leaf Arena, in the city,' said the Queen. 'Unfortunately, that venue is needed for many shows throughout the year, so some kind of opera season would need to be established. They're also considering the Acrodryohydrus Opera House, but of course it has that name for a reason.'

'I wish there was something I could do,' said Cyril, sadly.

The carriage pulled up outside the opera house and the family stepped out, strolling towards the huge building. The opera house had a broad, cylindrical centre, with an onion-shaped spire and two church-like buildings on the sides. As Cyril's parents said it would be, it was all on the edge of a coastal cliff.

'You can't see the island from here, but it's getting closer every minute,' said the Queen. 'Let's just enjoy the evening while we can.'

They reached the main doors and were announced as they walked onto the red carpet by the entrance. Cyril gazed in wonder at the beauty of the building. There were pillars, stained glass windows, chandeliers and many other well-dressed people, and the whole building had been specially decorated with ribbons for this final evening.

'I find this environment extremely nostalgic,' said Cyril.

When it was time for the audience to be seated, the King, Queen and Cyril headed over to the royal box. From there they could see the orchestra and the large curtain that covered the activity on stage.

'I think you'll like this, Cyril,' said the Queen.

'The performance will be quite long,' said the King. 'You'll feel like a part of a story by the end.'

'I'm already part of a story,' said Cyril.

Members of the stage crew extinguished the torches on the walls, making the auditorium almost completely dark, and the chatter of the audience swiftly dwindled into silence. Moments later, music erupted from the orchestra pit, but the curtain stayed down.

'This is just the overture,' the Queen explained to Cyril. 'Basically, an instrumental introduction.'

The music finished after a few minutes and there was a momentary pause before more music started and the curtain went up. The stage was set with medieval archways, tapestries and statues – an artistic portrait of an ancient time – and was rapidly brought to life by a cast of opera singers, dressed in period pieces.

'This is impressive,' whispered Cyril. 'I remember seeing something like this a long time ago.'

'Do you remember the music as well?' asked the Queen.

'Probably,' said Cyril.

Before long, there came a ballet sequence, which immediately drew Cyril's attention; graceful women in graceful costumes refreshed even more of his memory. There were a few male dancers too, whose costumes were more streamlined.

'This puts me in mind of the paintings on our walls,' said Cyril. 'I seem to recall that Matthias had one resembling a scene like this.'

Cyril began to feel increasingly emotional and as he watched the climax of the ballet sequence, a single tear ran down his cheek.

'I cannot let this disaster happen,' he whispered to himself. 'The opera house must remain standing!'

The intermission came and the curtain fell, prompting the stage crew to relight the torches on the walls. The audience blinked themselves back into reality and resumed conversation as they started to file out of the auditorium. The royal family came out of their box, wandering down the fancy corridor towards the foyer.

'So, what sort of events do they host downstairs?' asked Cyril.

'They have a restaurant on one side of the theatre and a ballroom on the other,' said the Queen.

'We ordered our meal for the intermission,' said the King. 'We might have to wait a while, but it's a long time before Act II tonight.'

Shortly, the royals were enjoying a glass of wine at their large table in the restaurant wing and the King and Queen were chatting merrily away to some friends, who were sitting at the table with them. 'I regret that I was unable to eat with you at the previous party, but I shan't miss it this time,' said the Queen. 'Besides, tonight is far more meaningful.'

Cyril, at the other end of the table, was talking to some listeners of his own. He was resting his hand on the table, holding his knife.

'On those islands across the sea, I had to battle wolves and lions. And before that, I journeyed into the swamp forests and ended up victorious over a foul group of alligators.'

He dipped his knife into his red wine and licked it, shocking his listeners.

'You'll never know what you might have the urge to do when you're cheating death, as they say,' Cyril added.

Eventually, their dinner was served. Cyril caught sight of a roasted wild boar with an apple in its mouth and was a bit worried.

'I'm not sure I fancy the idea of eating dead animals anymore,' he said to no-one in particular. 'Where are the vegetables?'

Once they had finished their meal, Cyril decided to take a walk round the building. As he came strolling down the grand staircase, he bumped into Lydia.

'Y...Your Highness!' exclaimed Lydia.

'Lydia!' said Cyril.

Lydia was wearing a thin white balletic frock with gloves and a black neck band. She also had a flower in her hair and elegant slippers on her turned-out feet.

'Good evening,' said Cyril, regaining his composure.

He took Lydia's hand and kissed it. Lydia gently pulled

her hand away, looking nervous, and proceeded to wave her fan in front of her face as they walked down the stairs together.

'What brings you to the opera tonight, then?' asked Cyril.

'I'm here to see my siblings dance,' said Lydia. 'I won't have the opportunity to see them perform again for I don't know how long.'

'Oh, I'm sorry to hear that,' said Cyril.

'Yes…listen, Cyril…I'm sorry about that day on the ship,' said Lydia. 'I've thought through my actions, and it wasn't fair of me to simply leave you like that. Can you please forgive me?'

'I don't know what to think right now,' said Cyril. 'I'm under a spell almost. I don't feel like a child anymore. I feel like a fully-grown gentleman.'

'You are a grown gentleman, Cyril,' said Lydia, as they reached the bottom of the stairs.

Cyril turned to face Lydia and placed his hand under her chin, looking at her red crests.

'You blush in the most beautiful way, Lydia,' he said. 'You blush in the most beautiful way…'

Lydia smiled and reached up, as Cyril slowly kissed her on the lips. Lydia's tail coiled tightly in delight and her crests became so red they looked as if they were about to let off steam. Eventually, they pulled away from each other and Cyril looked adoringly into Lydia's eyes.

'Do you…by any chance…' said Cyril. '…feel like dancing again?'

A moment later, they were dancing in the ballroom wing, under the light of a glistening chandelier. They were standing close together, turning slowly on the spot in time to the music and talking all the while.

'I have to confess,' said Lydia. 'It took my siblings a lot of quarrelling with our parents before they finally allowed them to take to the stage.'

'I'm not surprised, it looks terrifying,' said Cyril.

'I actually went to ballet school with them for a while,' said Lydia. 'In fact, it was I who encouraged them to dance. When they saw me dancing, they wanted to do it themselves and they were far more suited to it than I was. That's why I left. I didn't want them to feel embarrassed by me, not to mention I was terrified of the mistresses. But it's strange to think…my siblings wouldn't be here if I hadn't given them the…the motivation…'

She hugged Cyril as she started to sob.

'Yes, I know, it's an emotional evening for most of us,' said Cyril. 'Just think, we wouldn't even be able to dance without these vertical backbones, would we?'

Lydia dried her tears and looked at him. 'No, I suppose not. Well, if this is to be my last dance in this ballroom, having a prince for my partner is more than I deserve.'

They danced over to a row of windows on one side of the ballroom and stopped to look outside. The sky was growing darker and guards had begun to light the beacons.

'It's so beautiful,' sighed Lydia.

Cyril could just make out the incoming island, sitting out in the open sea, not far from the mainland. 'So that's the island that will strike the cliff? A bit like a ship striking the rocks and sinking, but in reverse?'

'Pardon me, Your Highness,' came a voice from behind them.

They turned to see Vincent the artist, wearing a long, golden coat.

'Mr Verccito!' Cyril shook his hand. 'How are things with you, may I ask?'

Vincent talked inanely with them for a minute before bringing the conversation round to what he really wanted to discuss.

'It may be too late, Your Highness, but the carpenters tell me they could build a vital weapon to force the island away from the mainland. I've been working on a diagram and have made some calculations of the size and force such a tool would require. Might I discuss it with you tomorrow?'

'That sounds like an excellent idea,' said Cyril. 'We can meet in the North-West Forest town square around midday and I will take you to my cousin's house. He's a carpenter and a wooden structure designer, so he may be of some help.' Cyril turned to Lydia. 'It's not over yet. Vincent and I will see what we can plan tomorrow. But first, I must get a better view of that island.'

Cyril hastily made his way back up the stairs to where his parents were standing, jogging straight past them.

'Cyril, where are you going?' asked the Queen.

'To the roof!' he yelled back, not stopping to turn around.

The confused King and Queen followed him up the stairway and out onto the balcony, which ran around the outside of the opera house. Cyril smiled. The island was much clearer from there.

'Are you still trying to say your goodbyes to this place?' asked the King.

'Not yet,' said Cyril. 'Not without a struggle…'

The next day, Cyril and Vincent met in the main square of the small town in the North-West Forest. The town was comprised mostly of small, humble houses with flowerbeds and featured a fountain in the centre of the town square. In the small town lived Cousin Fergus, who had a particularly large house compared to the others, made of wooden beams and a workshop right next to it.

Cyril and Vincent were soon knocking on his door and Fergus swiftly came out to meet them, wearing his waistcoat and tights rather than his apron and work clothes.

'Hello, Cyril,' he said.

'I hope I'm not disturbing you,' said Cyril.

'No, not at all, I was just about to have a bite to eat,' said Fergus. 'How have you felt since the royal party?'

'Oh, much better, especially since the opera last night,' said Cyril. 'This is Vincent Verccito, who was at the opera with me.'

Vincent and Fergus shook hands.

'So, you were at the royal party too were you, Mr Verccito?' said Fergus.

'I was,' said Vincent. 'I have here a plan that we would like to discuss with you, if you would be so kind.'

'It's to do with the nearby island off the West coast and

its collision course,' said Cyril. 'We might just have worked out how to stop the island in its tracks.'

'This sounds interesting. Come in and I'll make you a cup of tea,' said Fergus.

Whilst drinking their tea at his kitchen table, Cyril and Vincent laid out the diagram for Fergus to look at.

'So that's what we need to do,' said Cyril. 'Build a giant battering ram. We'll need lots of wood to build it.'

'This is more than a small favour you're asking of me,' said Fergus.

'But surely, half of the task is designing the contraption,' said Vincent. 'And I've already done that. Now all we need to do is the construction part.'

'Are you certain this is a good idea?' asked Fergus. 'Why not simply let nature take its course?'

'With forward-facing eyes and opposable thumbs, we have the ability to plan and to design, and we have extraordinary construction skills,' said Vincent. 'We've been shaping the world around us, and increasing our chances of further success, for generations.'

'Yes, we should go through with it,' said Cyril. 'Besides, I want to show my parents how grown-up I am.' He dipped his head and continued to talk slowly. 'This island is going to collide with the coast and destroy the opera house on the cliff, meaning they may not be able to go to the opera for a very long time. I desperately want to do them a favour. I hardly kept my eyes shut last night thinking about it. I kept strolling round the outside of my tree, waiting for the grass to get wet. You must help me, Fergus.'

'Very well, I will see what I can do,' said Fergus.

Over the next few days, Vincent and Cyril sent out leaflets to people all across the Kingdom, asking if they would be willing to assist in the building of the giant battering ram. They went around the North-West town first, then the city and then visited the people living alone in the countryside. Horse-drawn timber wagons were acquired, to carry logs and felled trees from the forest.

At the end of the week, all the volunteers met on the beach below the opera house. For this task, Cyril was wearing plain expendable outdoor clothes, more like those worn by farmers than his usual royal garb. He stood with his back to the waves and addressed the crowd:

'Your attention, please. You have all been summoned here to assist in the construction of a vital weapon. As you know, the island behind me is due to smash into this very coastline and cause an unspeakable deal of damage. This must not happen. Thus, we have decided to build a battering ram, to counter the island's attack. It will take several days, but lunch will be provided, and in return for your co-operation, I will arrange a group holiday for you all to Acrodryohydrus Island next week. Mr Verccito, if you please...'

Vincent stepped out of the crowd. 'Thank you, Your Highness. This is the plan...' He gathered the crowd around the upsized drawing he had made of his original diagram, using a stick to draw in the sand, and explained how they would go about building the battering ram.

Soon, everybody was hard at work, measuring, sawing wood and fitting blocks together. Vincent and Mel Blue-Bottom were working near each other, on the frame of the huge structure.

'Mr Blue-Bottom?' said Vincent.

Mel turned to him.

'I'm glad to see *you're* involved,' said Vincent. 'Do you understand now the abilities we people have which animals do not?'

'There are tribes of wild people in the forests and jungles, you know,' said Mel. 'They'd have done this job just as well as us.'

'You don't imagine that Prince Cyril would honestly want help from those creatures, do you?' asked Vincent. 'It's possible that we'll look back on this memorable occasion, and if by chance you were to write about it, I would gladly do some drawings. Just as long as you're willing to acknowledge that our place stands above that of animals.'

'Of course,' sighed Mel.

Lydia was at the gathering too, dressed in a warm coat, trousers and boots. She was in charge of providing lunch for all the workers, and the witches had volunteered to bring their cauldrons along and do most of the cooking. They were not dressed as they usually were either; they too wore trousers, boots and thick coats, and they were not wearing their hats, though their clothes were still black.

Lydia saw the pink-eyed witch take a crab off the sand and over to the cauldrons. 'Stop! We agreed no seafood.'

'It's for us,' said the tailed witch.

'Yes,' said the pink-eyed witch. 'What about *our* lunch?'

'You should start cooking our lunch after everyone else's,' said Lydia.

'But it may take a while to hunt enough crabs for the full meal,' said the pointy-eared witch.

'Just don't mix them up,' said Lydia. 'Not everyone has a diet like yours…or mine,' she added as she turned round to face the table.

A long lunch table had been set up further along the beach, under a canopy, and the witches and Lydia quickly filled it with the food they had made, before calling all the workers over. The tide began to creep up the beach as the workers ate their lunch, but fortunately the table was far enough away to avoid getting wet. Cyril was sitting opposite Vincent, who had finished his lunch and was busy drawing.

'Vincent, what are you up to?'

'I'm drawing what we've built of the weapon so far, in case we wish to look back on it,' said Vincent. 'When the battering ram is finished and approved, I'll know once and for all how great a force we people are.'

'Well, I think you've been very helpful indeed, Vincent,' said Cyril. 'It has to be said this was *your* idea. When it has proven its power, I suppose we'll both have put our minds at rest.'

By the afternoon, two days later, the work was done. The battering ram had a four-legged frame and there was a mass of tied-together tree trunks hanging on chains from the frame. Two extra chains were attached to the end of the trunks, facing the cliff and leading up onto the grass. The island, of course, was not far away.

Cyril addressed the workers. 'Thank you, people. You have all been most co-operative. We will see the power of this beauty when the time comes. I will send up a red firework when I need your help and strength. Those of you who are coming back to help me swing this giant contraption, be constantly on the lookout for fireworks. Those who are not, we will let you know the result as soon as possible. Regardless of how this turns out, I will still ensure that all of you have the chance to go on that holiday I promised. You are free to go now.'

All the workers and volunteers started to leave the beach as Cyril walked over to the battering ram, admiring the huge weapon. His parents were there and they came up alongside him.

'How do you feel about this, Cyril?' asked the Queen.

'It *has* to work,' said Cyril.

'I think you've done a pretty good job of it either way,' said the King.

'Make sure you take one last look at that opera house,' said the Queen. 'Just in case.'

While most of the volunteers were staying in a camp in the North-West Forest town, Cyril had found accommodation where the cast and crew of the operas usually stayed, high up in the opera house itself. Each morning, he looked out of the window to see the island drawing ever closer. When he felt it was time to try and push the island away, he sent up red fireworks, signalling for everyone to come and help. They all hoisted the battering ram by its two extra chains on the cliff, then, on Cyril's command, they let go of the chains, attempting to generate enough force to push away the island.

One afternoon, as another firework was launched on the West coast, a large shadow fell over the city to the East, causing panic and chaos. The city was quickly evacuated, as jets of flame swept through the lanes between the houses...

The island was directly drifting towards the coast now, and a collision looked certain as the waves grew larger, almost reaching the top of the cliff edge. Cyril had the battering ram make one more violent strike, before the island drifted too close, but to no avail.

'RUN!' screamed Cyril.

The island crashed into the cliff with so much force that the back wall of the opera house crumbled and the stage collapsed in an echo of rumbling and smashing. Small forest animals scampered off the island and onto the mainland, eagerly exploring their new home. Cyril was the first to survey the ruins and was devastated by the damage. He could see the trees beyond the destroyed back wall. This was not stage scenery; the trees, sky, and animals were real.

'Gaaah!' he yelled. 'This cannot be happening!'

The deer and squirrels from the island continued to scramble over the debris, but Cyril chased them away.

'Get out of this building, all of you!' he shouted as they fled through the doors.

Lydia appeared, up in the balcony of the theatre behind him. She was shocked to see the new, very real forest round the back of the auditorium and to observe Cyril's aggressive behaviour. As Cyril made his way towards the doors of the auditorium, Lydia made her way back downstairs, and they spotted each other as Cyril entered the foyer.

'Cyril!' Lydia cried, running down the ruined staircase.

Cyril looked up. 'Lydia?'

They came up to one another and hugged tightly for a while, as plaster continuously fell from the ceiling.

'You're so tense,' said Lydia. 'Are you alright?'

'I feel so ashamed, so…embarrassed,' said Cyril. 'I feel like I let everyone down, my parents most of all.'

'Cyril,' said Lydia. 'It was a very good try. You did mean well, and in some ways your intensions mean as much as your actions. But this time it was beyond your control. What difference could you have made?'

Cyril thought for a moment.

'I think maybe you should go home and explain to your parents what happened,' said Lydia. 'They'll understand.'

'No, they won't,' said Cyril. 'I can't show my face there again.'

'Cyril, it wasn't your fault,' said Lydia. 'Your parents never asked you to save the building.'

'I only wanted to stop it from happening, and to prove myself,' said Cyril. He then gave a sigh. 'Fine. I will go back. I will tell my parents the truth.'

'Good man,' said Lydia.

At that moment, E.V. came into the foyer.

'Oh, Your Highness,' she said.

'E.V was helping with the construction,' said Lydia. 'She's also been helping attend to the injured.'

'I heard a lot of noise coming from in here and was wondering what had happened,' said E.V.

'It's alright,' said Cyril. 'I was just annoyed with the whole thing. But thanks anyway, E.V.'

He gave her a big hug.

'Oh…thank you, Cyril,' said E.V. slightly uncomfortable.

Cyril let go of her.

'Now listen, both of you,' said E.V, as the plaster fell. 'The subsidence is affecting the cliff edge and it could give way at any moment.'

'Come on, then,' said Cyril. 'We'd best get out of here!'

The three of them abandoned the foyer, rushing out of the building and through the gateway. The opera house was not collapsing, but it did appear to be sinking into the ground.

'It could take days for it to crumble completely,' said Lydia.

'We should just go back home, then,' said Cyril.

'Yes, and I may have some patients to treat,' said E.V.

She made her way towards the crowd of volunteers who were journeying back to the city.

'Do you want me to come with you?' Lydia asked Cyril.

'No, no. But I am grateful for your help. Here, I want to lend you this.' Cyril took off his ring and gave it to her.

'The Prince's Ring?' said Lydia.

'That's the first time I've taken it off since that night at the opera,' said Cyril. 'I wanted to keep it on, to remember my promise, the promise of saving this theatre. But now it has a new purpose. If you ever need my help, come to my home and show the ring to the guards, telling them I gave it to you.'

'Thank you,' said Lydia, slipping on the ring.

She began to walk back down the hill towards the retreating crowd.

'Lydia?' said Cyril.

Lydia looked back.

'Thank *you*,' said Cyril. 'And have a nice stay on Acrodryohydrus Island.'

When Lydia returned to the city, she was shocked to find that much of it had been burnt down. Instead of market traders, the city was packed with crowds of traumatised homeowners, sitting on the pavements being consoled by the royal army.

'What happened?' Lydia asked one of the soldiers.

'There's been a dragon attack, Madam,' said the soldier. 'You might want to make your way to the Emergency Accommodation Centre.'

'That won't be necessary.'

Lydia continued walking, in the direction of her inn, but as she turned the corner, she went from shocked to horrified and dropped to her knees. Her inn had been burnt to a cinder.

Some of her staff were outside, crying and injured, and

when two of them saw her, they came over.

'Miss Lydia!' wailed one of them.

'We've been so worried,' sobbed the other. 'I'm sorry you have to see this.'

'I…I don't know what…what to say,' stuttered Lydia, with her hand over her mouth.

Her two staff members comforted her, putting their arms around her shoulders. 'Don't worry Miss, we can take you to the accommodation centre.'

'No, no need,' said Lydia. 'I know exactly where to go. Could you just leave me alone for a moment?'

Once they had left, she looked down at the ring on her finger.

'Bless you, Cyril!' she said quietly.

After searching through the rubble for a moment, she headed down the main road and into the forest, away from the city towards the countryside, wearing her best cloak and white gloves. Just as she approached a wooden destination sign, she heard a loud rustling in the undergrowth and immediately hid behind a tree. A microdraconyx burst into her intended path, growling softly as Lydia's smell drew it slowly towards the tree. Lydia's heart was beating violently, but the lizard suddenly looked up, distracted by what sounded like gunshots coming from the direction of the city. To Lydia's relief, the creature galloped straight past her hiding place, off to investigate the noise. Lydia knew it was probably the military, preparing for more intruders, and she cautiously continued towards the sign ahead.

It was evening by the time Lydia arrived at Cyril's home, and she was exhausted, mustering just enough energy to drag herself slowly to the main gates and show Cyril's ring to the guards.

Meanwhile, Cyril was having dinner with his parents in the dining room.

'I just can't believe I couldn't do anything about it,' he said. 'The first time I've actually wanted to do you a favour, and I didn't succeed.'

'But you did take charge of a whole group of people, in order to carry out an otherwise triumphant task,' said the Queen. 'That battering ram was truly something to behold while it lasted.'

'Yes, but so too was the Architectural Armageddon,' said Cyril. 'The idea I've given you of how I might take command in the future is clearly terrible, isn't it? I failed the test.'

'You did not fail the test,' said the King. 'Failure is the most important lesson.'

'You mean *guilt* is the most important lesson,' muttered Cyril.

'No, that's not what I mean,' said the King. 'We're perfectly willing to give you more chances.'

'More chances to fail?' said Cyril.

'Chances to learn from your mistakes,' said the Queen. 'And right now, your biggest mistake is blaming yourself.'

'I can't help but feel ashamed,' said Cyril.

The Queen kissed him on the forehead, just as Reginald appeared at the doors.

'Majesties? There's a young lady who wishes to see His

Highness. She has The Prince's Ring.'

'Lydia!' cried Cyril, as he stood up and ran from the room.

The King and Queen looked at each other, clueless as to what was going on.

'I wonder what he's done this time,' said the Queen.

'I thought he was more likely to fall in love with E.V.,' said the King. 'They have a lot in common.'

A short while later, Cyril brought Lydia into the dining room and gave her a goblet of water, as she sat down and began to tell them what had happened.

'Why, that's simply awful,' said the Queen.

'I did see the disaster zone, Ma'am,' said Lydia. 'But I'm only speaking of what they told me about the dragon attack. There's no telling where these dragons are now, or indeed how many of them there are. Soldiers are guarding the city and people are being looked after at the Emergency Accommodation Centre, but it doesn't feel safe in the city anymore.'

'I understand, Miss Lydia,' said the Queen.

'This may not be the best time to talk about it,' said Cyril. 'But how are the holiday arrangements coming along?'

'Well, nobody seems interested anymore after what's happened,' said Lydia. 'If anything, the children want to go instead.'

'You know, that might not be such a bad thing,' said Cyril. 'If this carnage gets any worse, we'll need to evacuate all the young children, and a safe haven like

Acrodryohydrus Island would be the perfect place. We can keep them there until this whole situation is behind us.'

'I agree,' said the Queen. 'Those children are the future. It is vital that we keep them safe, away from this disaster zone. Some of our wealthiest citizens live on the island, so I'm sure they would be willing to accommodate the children if need be. We can think on it more tomorrow. For the time being, Cyril, why don't you show Lydia to the guest room?'

'Can I show her my room first?' asked Cyril.

'Yes, that you can do,' said the King.

'But first, have her change into some more appropriate clothing,' said the Queen. She turned to Lydia. 'Our maid, Nancy should be able to assist you.'

'Is that really necessary?' asked Cyril. 'She looks so humble and soothing in her current outfit.'

'Yes, but I guarantee that a dress would be far more soothing for Lydia's own physical comfort after her long hike,' said the Queen. 'Do you agree, Miss Lydia?'

'Absolutely, Ma'am.'

Nancy soon found a suitable dress for Lydia, and although it did not have a sleeve at the back for her tail, Lydia still managed to make the dress look like it had been made specially for her. Cyril showed her up the stairs to his bedroom, using the light of a single candle to guide their way. As Cyril opened the door, Lydia eagerly entered the room, fascinated to see what the Prince's bedroom looked like. She gazed in wonder at the colourful leaves and branches, twisted in intricate patterns, made more magical by the flickering candlelight.

'I feel like I'm dreaming, Cyril,' she said.

'So do I,' replied Cyril, taking off his shoes and waistcoat and coming over to join her. 'To have you, Lydia, in my bedroom – my comfort zone – is more than I deserve.'

He put his hand on Lydia's shoulder before she started sniffling.

'Is that snake repellent bothering you?' asked Cyril, concerned.

'No, it doesn't smell bad,' said Lydia. 'It's just a little strong.' She smiled. 'I have to admit, I must agree, to an extent, with your comments on my clothing earlier. As I have told my parents, time and time again, a change of clothes does not change a personality, even for a lady.'

'My parents would understand what you're saying,' said Cyril. 'It must be disappointing for them, to realise that we've grown up to become not exactly what they had expected.' He sat down on his bed, surrounded by his toys and books. 'I never grew out of these toys. They've always meant so much to me.'

He looked at Lydia and patted the space beside him, encouraging her to come over. She immediately came and sat next to him.

'I won't need this for much longer, Lydia,' said Cyril. 'But would you mind reading me one of these stories? You have such a voice, that I shall certainly fall asleep easily listening to you read.'

'Of course,' said Lydia fondly.

CHAPTER VII
BIG EQUALS VULNERABLE

Cyril had decided to meet up with Lawrence to find out if he knew anything about the destruction of the city and so, early the next morning, he and Finnegan set off towards his laboratory. When they arrived, the house was still locked and barred.

'He *is* in a cage then,' said Cyril. 'This is what he spent our money on when we bribed him.'

Cyril climbed off Finnegan and walked up to the gate, opening it with the keys Lawrence had given them. Hearing the bolt click, Lawrence opened the front door.

'Oh, Your Highness, I'm so glad you've recovered,' said Lawrence.

'I'm sorry I was so reckless,' said Cyril. 'There's another matter we need to discuss.'

'I think there is.'

Lawrence ushered Cyril inside and they were soon sitting at the dining room table.

'We tried everything we could,' Cyril was saying. 'But the battering ram was destroyed along with the opera house, and now the animals from that island have moved onto the mainland.'

'I had no idea you were even attempting this,' said Lawrence. 'You do realise that you can't change nature?'

'I still have much to learn, don't I?' sighed Cyril. 'But we're not here to discuss my mistakes. The real reason I came is to tell you that, around the same time as we were trying to save the opera house, half of the city was burnt. I hear it was a dragon attack, and witnesses have said that these dragons were vastly different to the ones we saw in the Reptile Kingdom.'

'It all adds up…' said Lawrence, sadly. 'I know you meant well but, unfortunately, because so many people turned their attention to helping you, they set the Kingdom out of balance. You see, Cyril, our Kingdom is simply a map on a page, and this imbalance you triggered caused the pages of time which make up our universe to fan. This will have enabled a whole group of immature animals, including those dragons, to climb up here, into our Kingdom, onto this map. Those dragons could be anywhere by now – as could whatever other creatures climbed up here for that matter – attempting to overthrow the Kingdom.'

'It's obviously a catastrophe,' exclaimed Cyril. 'Not only was all our hard construction work in vain, but I've put us all in danger!'

'I'm sure the soldiers will take good care of everyone,' said Lawrence. 'That's what they're here for, to protect us.'

'But I owe it to my parents,' said Cyril. 'I've got to do something about this. I have to earn their forgiveness.'

'If you really want their forgiveness, Cyril, just ask for it.'

'There's too much talking involved in that,' said Cyril. 'I need to prove myself to them.'

That afternoon, the King and Queen were sitting in their armchairs in the living room, watching Cyril pace up and down the wooden floor.

'I failed you once. I refuse to let it happen again. I will do something,' declared Cyril.

'Cyril, please don't be under the impression that you've failed us,' said the Queen.

'You still live with us, we have to take *some* responsibility for you,' said the King.

'I want to make it up to you one way or another,' Cyril insisted. 'I'm going to visit the centaurs, to see if they can come up with any ideas. I'll be back in time for dinner.'

As Cyril left the room, the Queen held the King's hand tightly.

'We can't keep him in this tree forever,' sighed the King. 'We've always wanted him to be more mature and understand what it means to be responsible.'

'But this was not what we had in mind, not this soon

at least,' said the Queen, her voice full of worry. 'He's continuing to put his life in real danger.'

As Cyril and Finnegan galloped to a halt in the middle of the herd of centaurs, Cyril noticed that most of them were not standing so proudly anymore. It was clear that the dragons had already made their mark.

'Good afternoon, centaurs,' said Cyril. 'I have been informed that a group of dragons are on the loose.'

'That is true, Your Highness,' said one of the centaurs.

'Lives, as well as our surroundings, have been lost,' said another.

They turned their heads towards a forest of burnt-down trees on a mountain side. Cyril looked at the sad scene and climbed down from Finnegan.

'Fear not, for I feel the same as you. The damage caused by these dragons cannot be tolerated. So, I have come up with a plan…'

All the centaurs sat down to listen to Cyril as he told them what Lawrence had told *him*, and what he had told his parents.

'The question is, how many of you would be willing to fight these dragons with me?'

'It would be a pleasure for all of us, excluding the women, children and the injured ones, to help you, Your Highness,' said one of the centaurs. 'Fighting is our speciality.'

'I shan't need you for anything else,' said Cyril. 'I just need bold warriors.'

The King and Queen's soldiers, along with those who served Prince Matthias, had volunteered to surround the city and guard it against further danger, and as night fell they looked up to the skies, awaiting another attack. Armed with swords, bayonets and canons, they were a vision of hope and heroism.

At the harbour, sailing boats were filling with children and departing, bound for Acrodryohydrus Island. It was a melancholy evening. The youngest children looked confused, as they said goodbye to their sad parents on the quayside, clinging to their older siblings and cuddly toys as they boarded the ships. They were all shepherded onto the boats by the oldest children, all girls in their late teens. The older boys who had just left school had been asked to stay and help defend the city.

Lydia was staying at Hugo and Henry's Hall, her old home in the city, and had acquired herself a temporary job in the restaurant while her inn was being rebuilt. As darkness crept over the city, the restaurant became busier, as regular customers came by for their evening meal; Mel Blue-Bottom, Vincent Verccito, the three witches and E.V. were all there for meals of their own, sitting at different tables. Mel and Vincent happened to be sitting at the same table and were discussing the recent battering ram incident.

'I had such high hopes that the battering ram would work,' said Vincent sadly.

'To tell you the truth, so did I,' said Mel. 'Where did we go wrong?'

'Nowhere. We just couldn't control the inevitability of nature. I suppose it is because we ourselves *are* a part of nature. I do feel sorry for the Prince though.'

Just then, the doors of the restaurant opened, and in walked Cyril. Everyone looked up at him and immediately stood to attention.

'Evening, everybody,' said Cyril. 'Please, be seated.'

As the diners all returned to their seats, Lydia, dressed as the other waitresses in a black waistcoat, black dress and light blue shirt, walked over to Cyril and greeted him. She had also had her hair cut round the neck and it was therefore untied.

'Good evening, Your Highness,' she said. 'Would you like me to show you to a table?'

'Oh, I've already had my dinner,' said Cyril. 'I came here to let you know—'

He stopped, looking around suspiciously, and led Lydia into a narrow, wooden walkway on the other side of the dining hall. It was so dark they could barely see each other's faces.

'You are aware that the mainland has been safely cleared of children by now?' enquired Cyril.

'Yes, I had heard,' said Lydia.

'I'm going into battle tomorrow,' Cyril told her. 'I've summoned a herd of centaurs to help me bring down those dragons.'

'Cyril, please don't do this,' begged Lydia, holding his hands. 'You'll kill yourself.'

'Don't worry, they are only immature dragons.'

'Have you even seen them?'

'No, not exactly. But we've seen the damage they are capable of causing which gives us a vague idea of their overall capabilities.'

'You shouldn't put yourself in such danger,' said Lydia. 'Your parents have spent your whole life raising you and to damage that life now would be selfish. You may be a man now, but you're still their precious child.'

'It's fortunate that they don't know I'm doing it then, isn't it?'

'You mean, you haven't told them about your plan to hunt the dragons?'

'How could I?' said Cyril.

Lydia dropped to her knees. 'At least let me, Lawrence and some of our other friends come and help. You'll need every vital skill to handle this ordeal.'

'But none of you are violent enough. It's too extreme a task. The centaurs were virtually born to fight, so they will do, but I could never ask you all for your help. I love you, Lydia. I don't want to lose you.'

He kissed her softly on the lips and they held each other tightly for a moment, before heading back into the light of the restaurant, the light revealing tears Lydia was shedding. Cyril gave her one final glance, smiling fondly, before walking through the restaurant doors and out into the night. Lydia came over to where her friends were eating their dinner.

Standing where they could all see her, she made an announcement. 'Mel, E.V., Vincent, Witches? Who here will help me to save the Prince from making a terrible mistake tomorrow?'

The next day, Cyril, dressed in a thick coat and boots, once again rode to the home of the centaurs. The adult centaurs were lined up, bows and arrows at the ready, when he arrived. After briefly greeting them all, Cyril raised his sword above his head and Finnegan reared dramatically.

'Let's go hunt down some dragon!' Cyril cried. 'Show them no mercy!'

He led the army of centaurs up into the mountains, leaving the women, children and the injured to watch them disappear.

Lydia, meanwhile, dressed in her coat, trousers and boots, had gathered all her friends together and brought them to the edge of the forest, just outside the city.

'Lydia?' Vincent asked. 'How exactly are we going to fight these things when we don't have any weaponry?'

'We're not fighting,' said Lydia. 'Cyril is, and he's got a herd of centaurs with him. We just need to find him to provide support. But for good measure…' She took a pistol out of her pocket. 'I smuggled this out of my father's house. He never uses the confounded thing now anyway, so he shan't miss it.'

'You're lucky the soldiers can't hear us,' said Vincent.

'Yes, I think we should leave this to the trained professionals,' said Mel.

'Now, hold on,' said Lydia defiantly. 'While most of the young children have been evacuated, all males who have finished secondary education have been left here, to join the military if the worst comes to the worst during this animal invasion. The soldiers just don't have the manpower to do this alone, and if they must, they will knowingly put those teenagers in danger. Honestly, the discipline in schools is harsh enough. We've got to protect not only Cyril, but all those other young men who still have their whole lives ahead of them. Besides, they too are on the brink of maturity. They can't afford to deal with immature creatures now.'

'That's generous thinking,' said Vincent. 'But if the young men of this world can't fight them, then why should we be able to fair better?'

'For many decades now, the military have made the ludicrous assumption that they stand a better chance of victory if they have male warriors. But it takes more than brute force to succeed. It takes agility, speed, intellectual thinking, all traits which females possess, and indeed excel at. We also tend to confuse winning and losing with living and dying, and these are what I have been trying to make Cyril understand.'

'But why, Lydia, are you taking this so personally?'

'Because…because I love Cyril,' confessed Lydia. 'And I want him to survive this. Now, come on! Let's go!'

Cyril, by this time, was in the depths of the forest, on the other side to where Lydia and her friends had just entered. It seemed peaceful, with sunlight drifting through the leafy canopy and flowers and toadstools scattered over the forest floor, but Cyril and his army soon discovered that the peace was misleading.

'Your Highness, look,' said one of the centaurs, pointing to some rather large footprints imbedded in the leaf litter.

'Hmm, they can't be dragon footprints, can they?' said Cyril. 'How could there be dragons in the forest?'

'You are quite right, Your Highness,' said a centaur. 'No animal of such a size can enter this forest…except, maybe, from…'

There was a great roar from above and they all looked up, the centaurs all drawing their arrows in readiness. They could barely see it at first, as its bright green skin was the same colour as the trees, but they knew it had to be a dragon. As it drew closer, Cyril could see that this dragon was indeed nothing like the ones he had seen in the Kingdom of Reptiles. It was almost cartoonish in appearance, with vibrant green skin, big round eyes and hardly any surface features, not unlike the dragons in Cyril's story books.

As the dragon landed, the ground shook violently, enabling Lydia to hear the commotion from the other side of the forest.

'What was that?' she said.

'We're looking for dragons, aren't we?' said the pink-eyed witch.

Lydia scrambled up the tree-covered hill to their right, crouching as she reached the top, and peered through the bushes to see what was going on in the forested valley below.

The dragon stood with Cyril and the centaurs at its feet, gazing at them with menacing, downward-facing eyebrows.

'I command you to leave these woods and go back to where you came from!' said Cyril.

'You must be the one who has tried to forget about us,' said the dragon. 'We've been waiting for this day for a long time, the day when one of you would put the map out of balance and allow us to return. Are you not fond of us anymore?'

'I'll always look up to you, in more ways than one,' said Cyril.

'One way is enough,' said the dragon. 'I'm sorry, but we have already turned on you. We cannot undo what has been done.'

'Very well,' said Cyril. 'If that's the way you want it…fire!'

The centaurs opened fire, as did the dragon, prompting Finnegan to jump aside so fast that Cyril fell to the ground, crying out in pain as he was struck by some of the dragon's

169

burning red and yellow fire. The fire spread several miles through the forest but, fortunately, the centaur's arrows eventually scared the dragon off and it flew back into the sky. The centaurs, noticing Cyril lying on the ground, came to his aid. Some of his skin was pink and his coat was ruined, but he was still alive.

'Your Highness!' exclaimed one of the centaurs. 'Say something!'

'I forgot never to draw first blood,' said Cyril, weakly. 'Now they'll really hate me.'

'Are you alright?' asked another centaur.

'My skin feels awful,' moaned Cyril.

'I am not surprised, Your Highness,' said the first centaur. 'It is most unfortunate that we are miles from a doctor,' he added, unaware that E.V. and the rest of Lydia's group were in the same forest, not so far away.

The group had been heading in the direction of the commotion that Lydia had spotted from her vantage point, and they had just stopped to rest their legs and grab a bite to eat, beneath the shelter of a stone ledge. The witches had worked their magic with minimal ingredients, a small cauldron on strings and a wooden stand, and the groups were all enjoying a much needed helping of delicious soup.

'How much longer will we spend in these trees, Lydia?' asked the tailed witch.

'Just a few more minutes walking,' said Lydia. 'Then, if we're still without success, we'll head back to the city. We must be near the Western Mountains by now.'

The bushes started to rustle, and everybody turned

their heads in panic. Much to their relief, it was Lawrence who burst out. He was on foot without Sebastian.

'Lawrence!' exclaimed Lydia.

'Lydia?' said Lawrence. 'What are you lot doing out here? Let me guess, you've come looking for Cyril?'

'How did you know?'

'It's the very same reason *I've* come out here. Cyril will be in mortal danger if he doesn't have our help. Look, I've already been struck by dragon fire…' Lawrence showed them a nasty burn on his arm.

E.V. immediately stood up and came over to Lawrence, with her wooden case in hand.

'How bad is it, Lawrence?' she asked.

'It was on fire for about fifteen seconds,' Lawrence answered, as E.V. opened her case. It was filled with bandages, medicine bottles, medical instruments, containers filled with water and a flask of purified alcohol. She rummaged around, pulling out various items and began treating Lawrence's wound.

'Lydia?' said Vincent.

Lydia looked up from her lunch.

'There's something camouflaged over there.' Vincent pointed to a small opening in the forest, almost filled in by the branches of the trees. As they all peered through, they noticed what looked like an old castle, sitting atop a tiny island in the middle of a lake.

'That's the Western Mountain Castle,' said Mel. 'It's where the royal family used to live before these trees grew up around it. After that, it was abandoned and became part of the forest.'

But then, they heard the roar of more dragons.

'The castle…' said Lydia. 'Shall we make a dash for it?'

'But the bridge has been demolished,' said the pointy-eared witch. 'You didn't exactly enquire whether we would be willing to *walk on water* when you asked us to come with you on this excursion.'

'Can you all swim?' asked Lydia.

'Oh, dear…' Mel looked rather nervous. 'I'm not the man I was but…I think I still can…I suppose.'

They all hid their belongings in the undergrowth, removed their coats and ran over to the moat.

'Just dive straight in!' said Lydia as they neared the edge.

They followed her lead and immediately dived into the water, swimming swiftly over to the other side.

When they reached the island, the tailed witch made a suggestion. 'Why don't we stay in the water? The dragons wouldn't be able to burn us, would they?'

'It's alright, the castle was built to withstand worse than dragon fire,' said Lydia. 'Come on, let's find a doorway.'

The castle was old, and there were plants and a few tree branches growing through most of the windows, though some of the stained-glass windows were still intact. At first, the castle appeared to be a pale, rusty-brown colour, but on closer inspection they could see that it was made of cream-white marble.

'Wait here,' said Lydia.

She made her way cautiously up a flight of steps to a door and gently opened it, before immediately leaping backwards, horrified. A large centaur was standing in her path, aiming its bow directly at her.

'Don't shoot!' yelled Lydia in a panic. 'We've come here to hide from the dragons!'

Cyril was standing on the top of the castle behind the battlements, and he peeked over when he heard the noise.

'What's going on? Lydia?!'

'Cyril!' cried Lydia. 'I might have known!'

'I might have known too!' said Cyril. 'It's okay,' he told the centaur. 'Let them in.'

The centaur kindly stepped aside, allowing Lydia and her friends into the castle.

After drying themselves off a little, Vincent and Mel decided to explore the castle, wandering down a concrete passage and coming to a chamber with tall windows on one side. They looked out of one window.

'Can you see them anywhere?' asked Mel.

'I think I see two of them on the horizon,' said Vincent. He turned around to face the chamber. 'Whatever happened to this place? There are mice and grass snakes crossing these tiles and so much greenery is sneaking in.'

'If you think about it, this is not so different to the inside of the royal family's tree,' said Mel. 'The only difference is that this is a building, constructed by the hand of man.'

'It's as if this building is turning into a tree,' said Vincent. 'I imagine Cyril must feel at home here.'

'No doubt he does. I was thinking, you know, today's events would make an excellent article. Shall we produce one together?' asked Mel.

'That we could do,' said Vincent. 'But I don't have a drawing pad or pencil with me, so you'll have to give me a moment to memorise this room.'

'*Royal Home: From Castle to Tree*,' said Mel. 'How does that sound for an article title?'

'You do the writing; I'll do the art,' said Vincent. 'I'll need a closer look at those dragons too. They're vicious, yes, but would be so lovely to create a picture of.'

Meanwhile, Lydia and Cyril were both behind the battlements, and they gave each other a hug.

'Lydia, what are you doing here with our friends?' asked Cyril.

'I'm sorry, Cyril,' said Lydia. 'But I just couldn't let you do this without our help. What happened to your coat?'

'It got burnt. I have a few burns on my body too.'

'Oh, dear! E.V. might be able to do something about that, she's already fixed Lawrence's burns—'

'Not now,' exclaimed Cyril. 'Look!'

They spotted three dragons flying over the forest and the mountains and the whole company ducked when they started flying towards them.

'They're so big and powerful, aren't they?' whispered Cyril. 'I don't really know how bows and arrows will possibly bring them down.'

'I'll fire a warning shot…' Lydia took out her pistol from her trouser pocket, cocked it, pointed it at the sky and pulled the trigger, but it only spat out water. 'Oh, blast, the gunpowder must still be wet. You are right, the dragons are extremely powerful, so it will be a challenge for anyone or anything to stop them, apart from the dragons themselves of course. But the bigger they are, the easier it is to aim for them and they have very few places to hide. That makes them nonetheless vulnerable.'

'So, based on what you've just told me, what's the plan?' asked Cyril.

'Well, what was your plan before I turned up?'

Their conversation was interrupted as one of the enormous dragons perched itself on top of the battlements, right above Cyril and Lydia. It roared ferociously as the other dragons began to blow great waves of flame towards the castle.

'I can really feel that heat,' whispered Cyril.

'Quiet,' whispered Lydia. 'Just hand me your sword for a moment.'

Cyril handed her his sword, and with tremendous force, Lydia thrust the sword up into the dragon's thigh. The dragon was shocked and confused.

'Open fire!' yelled Cyril.

The centaurs immediately fired their arrows and Mel and Vincent rushed to the windows to see what was happening. Vincent's ears turned pink.

'I never would have thought it would end like this,' said Mel. 'Waiting to be taken from inside an old, abandoned castle.'

'Pull yourself together, man,' said Vincent. 'It's not the end just yet.'

The first dragon wobbled out of control and crashed into its fellow dragons like aerial dominoes. Frightened and wounded, all three dragons flew away from the

175

burning forest and into the sky, to the sound of a victorious cheer from everyone inside the castle.

Cyril took a moment to grab Lydia's hand and drag her to the castle stairwell.

'May I have my sword back?' requested Cyril.

Lydia gave it to him. 'One thing those harsh dance lessons taught me is the pain caused by a good blow to the thigh! Cyril…?'

Her smile disappeared as Cyril boxed her in against a wall, looking very serious.

'Just how were you planning on defending yourself without me?' he demanded. 'If I hadn't been here, at the castle, what would you have done? Were you going to stay submerged in that moat where the fire couldn't touch you?'

'Cyril, if you must know, I never wanted to fight. You were triumphant, I admit, and we would probably have been defeated if you hadn't been here. But you must understand that it requires more than force to win a battle.'

Cyril calmly stepped back from her. 'Like what?'

'Did you have anything to eat today?'

'Only my breakfast. Otherwise, no. Why?'

'I have some food in a bag that I left in the woods,' said Lydia. 'You're welcome to have some of it. You cannot fight a battle on an empty stomach. Now, what are we going to do about those burns of yours?'

'They are a bit uncomfortable,' said Cyril. 'I'll ask E.V. to look at them.'

'One last thing. Do you have an extensive knowledge

about the behaviour of these immature animals?' asked Lydia.

'N…no, I only know where they came from,' Cyril stuttered.

'Exactly,' said Lydia. 'If we all teamed up together, our friends and your centaurs would stand every chance of winning a battle.'

'I will consider it,' muttered Cyril.

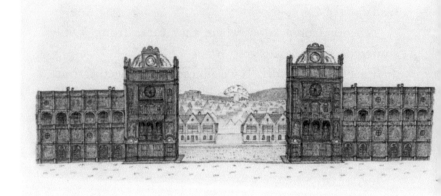

CHAPTER VIII
BEAUTY EQUALS DISTRACTION

It had been a week since Cyril and his centaurs had seen off the immature dragons, and once again Mel, Vincent, E.V., the witches and Lawrence were all having dinner at Hugo and Henry's Hall. Lydia was busy discussing the next plan with them as they ate.

'The Queen sent me a pigeon yesterday with a message, saying that Cyril was planning to go out again today.'

'Did the Queen happen to mention where?' asked Vincent.

'Well, she said he might try to see off those immature horse creatures that were spotted a few days ago. Goodness knows where they could be, or how many species there are. It will mean Cyril's centaurs have to face some of their own kind, but at least they'll all be herbivores this time. What do you think, Lawrence? Should we get involved?'

'They may be herbivores, but they will still be powerful creatures,' said Lawrence. 'Most members of the horse family can knock out the teeth of a big cat with a single kick. I think Cyril is going to need our help on this one. I'm quite happy to go if you are, Lydia.'

Cyril, meanwhile, was pacing around his living room ranting, while the King and Queen listened patiently from their chairs.

'Now, Cyril,' said the Queen. 'You've proven your heroism and your feelings for us. Do you think you could put your mind at rest now and leave the remaining work to the soldiers?'

'I've come too far to turn back now,' said Cyril. 'The remaining animals can't be much worse than those dragons.'

'Yes, they can,' said the King. 'What about those sea monsters the sailors have been talking about?'

'Hush!' said the Queen urgently.

'Oh, I'll find a way somehow,' said Cyril. 'Anyway, I'm only going to deal with the horses for the time being.'

'But you don't know how your centaurs, or Finnegan for that matter, may react to them,' said the Queen. 'I mean, they're all related. They might even have their own means of communication.'

'Then they can translate for me.' Cyril paced over to the portraits on the wall. 'I was never too bright, was I?'

'That was then, Cyril,' said the Queen. 'With

Lawrence's help, you have become a most intelligent and inquisitive son. But there are just a few more things you need to understand.'

Cyril turned around and raised his eyebrows at her. The Queen sighed.

'If you really want to go out again, fine. Just take care of yourself.'

'Something tells me I shouldn't really, but I want to…I have to. I'll be back for dinner.' Cyril came up to the Queen and kissed her on the forehead. 'You can trust me, Mum.'

'It's not *you* that I don't trust, Cyril. It's the rest of the world. Go on now, I'll see you later.'

Cyril turned and walked out of the room, leaving the Queen looking unhappy and the King standing beside his wife, holding her comfortingly.

A short while later, Cyril and Finnegan arrived back at the home of the centaurs and told them what the plan was.

'I don't want to worry my parents this time, so I told them I'd just try to track down these immature members of the horse family for now. Have any of them been sighted in these parts lately?'

'We have attempted to keep them away from our territory, Your Highness,' said one of the centaurs. 'There are unicorns and flying horses as well. The flying horses are easier to find, but more difficult to repel, since they spend most of their time airborne.'

'The unicorns normally roam the forest further east,' said another centaur.

'This should be interesting,' said Cyril. 'It will be quite something to see unicorns as I had always pictured them.'

On their journey east, away from the forest of the Western Mountains, Cyril and the centaurs had come across a vast woodland of small fruit trees. The trees were dainty and elegant, and their branches spread lazily out from their trunks, unlike in the Western Forest, where the trees were thick and gnarled, with branches that sprouted stiffly outwards.

'So, this is the orchard?' Finnegan remarked.

'Yes,' said Cyril. 'Apparently this is where we should find those unicorns.'

'I'm not surprised with all these apples and pears on the trees,' said Finnegan.

As they ventured out of the trees into a small, grassy glade in the middle of the forest, they came across two immature unicorns. One had a vibrant blue hide, and a yellow mane, while the other was purple in colouring, with a dark purple mane. They both had thick eyelashes and were very attractive.

'Wow, this really is something.' Cyril climbed off Finnegan but did not give the order to attack. He was too distracted by the glamour and bright colours of the two unicorns. 'Um…hello. These lands belong to other unicorns. Could you…possibly go back to where you came from?'

'Prince Cyril is it not?' asked the blue unicorn.

'Yes.'

'You've tried to let go of us, haven't you, Your Highness?' said the purple unicorn. 'That's why we've come to overthrow your world, to prevent you from forgetting us ever again.'

'Not likely,' said one of the centaurs. 'His Highness will give the order to take action soon enough.'

'No…' said Cyril. 'They're armed only with the horns on their heads. We can't just ruthlessly attack them. Remember what I said last time about drawing first blood?'

'Your Highness,' warned another centaur. 'You're being blinded by their appearance. We need to act now!'

At that moment, Lydia's group came charging out of the trees, frightening the unicorns away with sticks and stones. Cyril stared at them in surprise.

'You've got to be joking!' he said, as the unicorns retreated deeper into the orchard.

'Hello again, Cyril,' said Lydia.

'How did you know where I was?' asked Cyril.

'Your mother sent me a pigeon,' said Lydia.

'Blast, I forgot about the pigeons,' said Cyril. 'I don't need your help this time, Lydia. You just attacked first,

182

which is always a bad move, especially when they're only herbivores.'

'All right, all right. I won't do it again. I promise.'

Shadows moving on the orchard floor suddenly caught their attention, and they all looked up to see a herd of immature flying horses above them. The herd were a mixture of bright orange and pink, and nearly all of them had standing-up manes rather than flowing ones.

'Not *more* flying animals,' sighed Cyril.

'They're not landing down here,' said Lydia. 'It looks like they're heading for somewhere further away.'

'Come on, everybody,' said Cyril.

They headed further into the trees, following the shadows of the flying horses, but it was difficult for the centaurs to run in such dense woodland.

'Let's split up!' cried Cyril. 'I'll keep going this way. Lydia, you take that pathway there.'

On the edge of the forest stood a mansion, with a giant medallion hanging above its main doors decorated with images of horses. The mansion was used as a horse-riding campsite, featuring a large, black wooden barn around the back – which acted as shelter for the horses – and an extensive field of grass, with a track around it. Some of the horses were out in the field grazing, when an immature flying horse spotted them from the air and swooped down to land on the ground beside them.

'What's all this about?' asked one of the horses.

'You haven't seen a young prince by any chance, have you?' asked the flyer.

'A prince called Cyril?' asked another horse.

'Yes,' said the flyer.

'Not recently,' said the first horse.

'And even if we had, of what concern is it to *you*?' added the second horse.

Lydia's group, meanwhile, having been trekking through the woods for quite some time now, had stopped for a rest beside a gently trickling waterfall.

Lawrence was busy showing Lydia a book article about horses. 'We must be careful which unicorns or flying horses we repel. This is the area where most of them live, so we have to be able to tell them apart from the immature ones.'

'Lawrence,' said Lydia. 'Without a man of nature like you, the world would surely be lost. Even so, I cannot help but be afraid to deal with these animals.'

E.V. joined in with their conversation: 'All animals feel fear. You shouldn't be ashamed of it. The key is to use the fear your enemy creates against them.'

'But how do I do that?' asked Lydia.

'Show them you're not afraid of them...' E.V. guided Lydia to the ledge beside the waterfall and made her face the trees. 'Stand and walk as proudly as they do and try to turn those crests of yours red. The colour display will intimidate them.'

Lydia closed her eyes and thought very hard, managing to raise her blood pressure just enough to briefly flash her crests a brilliant red.

'It'll take time to perfect,' said Lawrence. 'But just keep

practicing; you'll soon be able to control that technique.'

'My parents brought me up teaching me not to do this with my crests,' said Lydia, eyes still closed. 'It's normally the males of my kind who use this ability. I've seen them turn their crests red when fighting over females…usually at taverns.'

The witches, meanwhile, had started to fire up their small cauldron a distance behind everyone else.

'It's your turn to get the fish,' said the tailed witch to the pointy-eared witch.

'Why don't we wait for good old horse meat?' asked the pointy-eared witch, licking her lips.

'There will be enough of that later,' said the pink-eyed witch. 'Now, go and fetch the fish.'

The pointy-eared witch grumbled to herself before walking down to the stream. She crouched down, rolled up her sleeves and began her attempt at fishing.

Lydia was still concentrating on her crests with the help of Lawrence and E.V. 'Ah, yes, I can hear the sound of my blood flow, splashing…splashing?' She opened her eyes and turned around to see the pointy-eared witch clasping a slippery fish.

'Hey!' she shouted, as she ran back across the ledge towards them. 'Stop! That's our only cooking pot and we don't all eat fish!'

'We're hungry though,' protested the tailed witch. 'And we don't know when we'll next have the chance to cook some delicious fish.'

'Oh, don't you worry,' said Lydia. 'Sooner or later, Cyril will lead us on a sea voyage; you can have plenty of fish when that time comes. Right now, though, we've got to move on.'

Cyril and his centaurs, on the other hand, hadn't stopped and were fast approaching the horse-riding campsite.

'There's the mansion,' said Cyril. 'My parents used to take me here every summer to practice horse riding.'

'Is this where we'll find the immature unicorns and flying horses then, Your Highness?' asked a centaur.

'Possibly,' said Cyril. 'A group of our horses live here, so I thought I'd ask them whether they've seen any of our immature friends.'

As they emerged from the trees, they saw a whole herd of brightly coloured immature unicorns, frolicking around the horse racing course.

'Come on, let's show them what we're made of,' said Cyril, making himself comfortable on Finnegan's back. 'You four come with me, and the rest of you chase them the other way until we've got them trapped.'

They began to stampede and Cyril took out his sword and held it high in the air, as the centaurs raised their arrows. Within moments, the unicorns were cornered.

'Did you really think I'd let you take over this countryside?' Cyril asked the unicorns.

'You may find that we're the ones who have *you* trapped, Your Highness,' said one of the unicorns mischievously.

From above, the herd of flying horses suddenly appeared and tried to scare Cyril and his centaurs away by kicking at them with their hooves. The centaurs, undeterred, opened fire, injuring some of the flyers. However, while this distraction was taking place, the unicorns seized their chance to jump off the track and into the centre of the circuit.

'Spread out around the track!' cried Cyril to the centaurs. 'We'll still have them cornered!'

Amidst the chaos, two tiny butlers, in their white shirts and black waistcoats, came out of the mansion to see what was happening.

'What the devil is going on here?' remarked one to the other.

'I think that's the young Prince over there,' said his companion. 'These must be some of the animals he's after.'

'Shall I send a pigeon to the soldiers?'

'I think that would be wise. I'll find some kind of weapon to get their attention in the meantime.'

Lydia and her friends were stunned by the commotion that greeted them when they finally made it out of the woods. They stared silently out at the mass of injured unicorns and flying horses as the fighting continued.

'Gracious!' exclaimed Lydia.

'I'd be careful if I were you,' Lawrence warned her. 'Those unicorn horns are dangerous, as are the hooves of the flying horses when in flight.'

'We need to put an end to this chaos,' Lydia exclaimed, shaken by the scene before her. 'I'll fire a warning shot.'

She took out her pistol and fired it into the air, and most of the fighters stopped to face her as she ran out from under the trees.

'Lydia!' exclaimed Cyril. 'You see, I have more people on my side than you think,' he shouted to the unicorns and the flyers.

'Leave the Prince alone, you immature creatures!' demanded Lydia. 'You may be gorgeous beings, but you can't persuade me to give in. I have faced and seen off monsters worse than you. I command you to surrender!'

The rest of Lydia's group had bravely come out of the forest and had formed a stubborn huddle behind her.

'I really don't want to harm you,' Lydia said, gently this time, putting her pistol away. 'Please, let us end this fighting.'

Cyril made a sudden movement with his sword and sliced the horn off a unicorn's head, uttering a gleeful battle cry as he did so. Much to Lydia's dismay, the fighting resumed.

'Quick!' Lydia heard a nearby voice say, and she turned to see one of the butlers, holding open the mansion's main door.

'In here!' he prompted.

Lydia and her friends nodded at one another and swiftly made their way inside, just as a pigeon flew out of one of the roof windows.

'You shouldn't be here,' said the butler. 'Who are you? Why have you come to this property?'

'I'm a good friend of the Prince's,' said Lydia. 'We're all his friends actually.'

'I see. Well, we haven't much time, but I think I could use you for a plan,' said the butler.

He quickly led them through the house to the rear and, when the back door was opened, they found themselves in the barn which was filled with horses in wooden pens. The back door and one side of the concrete mansion made up the fourth wall of the barn and it had been specially built as part of the house.

'How many of you can ride a horse?' asked the butler.

Lydia, Vincent, Lawrence and E.V. raised their hands.

'Get yourselves organised,' said the butler. 'I shall open the barn doors momentarily. As soon as I do so, you've got to ride out there immediately to aid the Prince.'

The four friends each opened a pen, climbed onto one of the horses and, as soon as the butler opened the barn doors, they rode out onto the field. The immature unicorns and flyers were surprised to see a group of fast horses charging towards them and began to flee. Lydia took out her pistol again as she galloped into battle. The horses were athletic enough to jump over the track barriers and send the unicorns running, and Lydia continuously fired warning shots as she made her way towards Cyril, ultimately scaring both the flyers and the unicorns away.

'Where did you learn to horse-ride, Lydia?' asked Cyril.

'Right here!' Lydia replied.

Cyril and his centaurs were completely worn out. Some of the centaurs had sustained bumps and bruises during the battle but, fortunately, all were alive. Several of the unicorns and flying horses had not been so lucky; their bodies lay on the track with arrows sticking through them, and where their eyes used to be there were now cross-

189

signs. Cyril jumped off Finnegan as Lydia came up to Cyril and hugged him.

'Why did you interrupt me and carry on the fighting, Cyril?' asked Lydia.

'You put away your pistol and I couldn't let the animals harm you,' said Cyril.

'You know, Cyril…' They sat down by the body of a flying horse as Lydia continued. 'I was standing up for you, trying to avoid more bloodshed. That's what friends are for. You have to let us help you, Cyril, and stand beside you to fight against the enemy together.'

'I wish I hadn't given the centaurs the order to fire,' sighed Cyril. 'Now they have to live with the shame of slaughtering their own kind, on my command.'

'It was self-defence,' said Lydia. 'It is instinctive for any animal to kill as a means of defence. You don't realise how ruthless you can be sometimes until you're in that situation, as you must have learnt by now.'

'Indeed, I have,' admitted Cyril, sadly. 'Even now, these poor animals are still things of beauty. I'll never forget them.'

'Don't make the mistake of judging things by their appearance, Cyril,' said Lydia.

Cyril slowly inched away from Lydia and drew his gaze away from her.

Then he stood up and walked over to Finnegan. 'Come on, Finnegan. Let's get back home for dinner.'

CHAPTER IX

TO REALISE WHAT GOES ON IN THE WATER

One evening, a few days later, Cyril was sitting alone having dinner in the Hugo and Henry restaurant. Lydia came out of the kitchen and sat down beside Cyril, and they discussed Cyril's next move.

'Yes, I'm going to confront the sea creatures tomorrow,' said Cyril. 'And there's not a lot you can do about it this time.'

'Cyril, you have no idea how dangerous animals in the water can be,' said Lydia. 'How do you plan on achieving such an insane task anyway?'

'I have access to the Royal Sailing Ship,' said Cyril. 'She's armed with cannons.'

'She's also been in your family for generations,' said Lydia. 'Your parents wouldn't want you to damage the magnificent vessel, would they?'

'That damage, as you call it, shall all be in the name of something good.'

'Cyril, just for a day or two, try to act like a civilian. Try to forget about all these animals and leave it to the professionals. That's what the royal soldiers are here for, to protect all of us.'

'I don't need protecting,' said Cyril. 'Have I not proven that?'

'Very well, Your Highness,' sighed Lydia. 'Be careful, and good luck.'

The next day, Cyril was giving the centaurs a brief explanation about the sea.

'What's it like out there, Your Highness?' asked one of the centaurs.

'That depends on the weather,' said Cyril. 'If the weather's rough, we'll drop anchor to keep the ship steady and, if absolutely necessary, there are cannons on the deck which we can use to defend ourselves and the ship.'

Unbeknownst to Cyril, Lydia's group were standing on the riverbank below E.V.'s bridge just outside the city, all kitted out in their countryside clothing, ready for their journey to the docks. They were also, on this occasion, wearing warm hats and scarves.

192

'So, how are you planning to help Cyril with this one?' Mel asked Lydia.

'The only possible way…' said Lydia. 'By hijacking a navy vessel.'

'Gosh, you've really changed,' said E.V. 'You don't mean it, do you?'

'I want to save Cyril from making his biggest mistake yet, and to be certain I get everything I require, I'm bringing along our old friend again,' she grinned, pulling her coat away from her body for a moment to reveal her old father's pistol tucked into her belt.

Cyril had already reached the dock and he and his army of centaurs were viewing it from the cliff edge, watching as ships were manoeuvred in and out of numerous wooden jetties and intersections designed to keep the ships separated.

'Look…all the ships are coming and going in that direction, to the right of us…always south.' said Cyril. 'They never travel straight forwards from the dock to the East, only for a minute or so to clear the harbour before turning right. Eastward must be where the immature sea creatures have been sighted. As you can see, there's a heavy military presence on the quay.'

Indeed, there were guards positioned all along the quayside, and cannons had been placed at regular intervals. The Royal Sailing Ship was there too, right where she had been moored after the last royal party.

'That purple one down there is our ship,' said Cyril. 'I would have brought you here the short way, but I had to look across the entire harbour to make sure she was still moored where we left her. Now, how to get down…'

Cyril glanced over the cliff edge. Ahead, there were a few black, wooden cabins, which were used to store fishing gear and seashells, positioned in rows upon a wooden platform, right on the edge of the cliff.

'Ah, yes,' said Cyril. 'I remember now. There's a staircase leading down to the harbour, just beyond those cabins. Let's go!'

They cautiously walked across to the platform, the centaurs slightly nervous about being too close to the cliff edge, and made their way down the staircase.

Inside one of the cabins, two fishermen were discussing the previous days catch over a couple of beers.

'Fishing out that swordfish was shocking enough,' said one of them.

'But when we saw those extraordinary mer-people, I thought the world had turned upside-down,' exclaimed the other. 'The sea is a weird old place.'

'What's happening out there?' his companion said, catching a glimpse of movement out of the window.

They both came over to the glass and were more than a little surprised to see a herd of centaurs, clip-clopping down the steps. They both looked at one another, mouths agape, before racing out of the cabin and peering over the edge of the cliff.

'Ay up!' one of the fishermen cried. 'What's your game then?'

The centaurs immediately raised their bows and arrows.

'Stop!' said Cyril. 'Lower your weapons! Stand down.'

'Are you the young Prince?' asked the first fisherman.

'I am,' said Cyril. 'I'm taking these centaurs on a special mission. I'm sorry if they startled you.'

'Quite alright, Your Highness,' said the other fisherman. 'We'll just leave you to it.'

When Cyril and the centaurs reached the Royal Sailing Ship, they wheeled the wooden ramp over to it, just underneath the side doors, and Cyril swiftly made his way up the ramp to open them. He stood atop the ramp and spoke to the centaurs.

'I am relying on you all. Serve the Kingdom and fight the enemy with me on this, your first sea voyage!'

The centaurs started to board the ship, fearful of the waves lapping against the side of it.

'No, Finnegan. You can't come,' said Cyril. 'You're too vulnerable.'

'But I gave your parents my word that I would always protect you!' Finnegan protested from the quayside.

'I'm aware of that, old friend,' said Cyril. 'I'll deal with my parents when we get back home, I promise.'

It was a bit of a struggle to convince the centaurs to shuffle their way down the wooden passages, up the wooden stairways and through the doors onto the main deck, but Cyril just about managed it. Standing on the deck, they looked out at the land and buildings in the distance.

'Well, here are your ultimate weapons for the day,' said

Cyril, proudly displaying the cannons.

'How do they work, Your Highness?' asked a centaur.

'Have you ever used matches?' asked Cyril. 'Or can you create fire with wood? Once you've loaded the cannon with a metal ball, hold a flame on top of this fuse and when it has burnt all the way down...BOOM! But remember, only use the cannons if and when I give the order.'

Cyril had the centaurs unfurl the sails as he headed up to the wheel. The centaurs found it difficult to stand up against the motion of the ship on the water but were able to maintain their footing as the ship made its way out of the port and into the open ocean.

By this time, Lydia and her friends had arrived at the top of the cliff and could see the Royal Sailing Ship out in the distance.

'Yes!' said Lydia. 'We've arrived early enough to see where they're heading.'

'Will they be alright in open water?' asked E.V. 'If the ship gets attacked and fills with water, there'll be nowhere to go but down.'

'Then we'd better get down there right away and chase after them!'

Lydia led them towards the wooden cabins and was just about to go down the steps, when the two fishermen stood in her way.

'Would you mind keeping away from this harbour, love?' said one of them.

'The young Prince has just set off on an important

assignment,' said the other.

'That's why I'm here,' said Lydia. 'And it's not an assignment at all, but a suicide mission. He's going to confront the immature sea creatures and is doomed if we don't go to his aid.'

'I'm sure the navy will take care of the situation now,' said one of the fishermen.

'The Prince knew the navy was out training on the other side of the island,' said Lydia. 'He knew what he was doing when he planned this. We've got to go and find Cyril fast, or it could take hours.'

'How's about you come into our cabin for a pint instead?' said the other fisherman.

Lydia took off her hat and turned her crests red, distracting the fishermen for a moment.

'You're Hugo's daughter, aren't you?'

'Yes.'

'Haven't seen your father in years. Let's have that drink, shall we? Talk about old times?'

Lydia nodded, allowing the fishermen to walk her over to the doors, before suddenly turning on them, yanking out her pistol and holding them both at gunpoint.

'Okay, people…' she said to her group. 'Hurry down to the quay, I'll catch up.'

As the rest of the group made their way down the steps, Lydia slowly backed away towards the steps, all the while keeping her eyes and her pistol fixed on the fishermen.

'I'm sorry to have to do this, but there's more to His Highness than meets the eye; we need to get down to that quayside. If you so much as try to follow us, I will not hesitate to use this, understand?'

She cocked her pistol at them to emphasise her point, and the two fishermen nodded nervously.

'Excellent. Thank you for letting me past.'

She turned swiftly and followed her friends down the steps, listening out for any sign of pursuit. But the fishermen had clearly heeded her warning and had decided to stay put.

As they reached the quayside, Finnegan came into view.

'Finnegan?' said Lydia, confused. 'Is that your name?'

'Yes, Lydia,' the horse replied, coming up to her and nuzzling her neck.

'Why are you still here at the dock?' asked Lydia.

'Cyril wouldn't let me go with him,' said Finnegan.

'Well, we can sort that out,' said Lydia, looking very determined. 'Come on.'

Finnegan and the rest of the group followed her down one of the jetties towards the H.M.S Charles, an enormous black naval vessel almost as large as the Royal Sailing Ship. Then just as they were about to climb aboard, two guards with rifles appeared, standing in their way.

Lydia held Finnegan by his bridle and spoke to the guards. 'Morning, gentlemen. This is the horse belonging to Prince Cyril, who just took that ship out into open water.'

'We are aware of that, lady,' said a guard.

'We'll make a rescue soon enough,' said the other.

'But the navy is miles away,' said Lydia. 'They'll never find him in time.'

'Do try and see it from my point of view,' said Finnegan. 'I promised the parents of the Prince…'

While Finnegan was distracting them, E.V. innocently came up alongside one of the guards; Lydia was already next to the other. Once E.V. was in position, Lydia nodded, and they both swung at the guards, punching them both below the belt, causing them to cry out in pain and enabling the two women to shove them off the jetty and into the water.

'Now!' yelled Lydia. 'All aboard!'

The guards were stunned, helpless and splashing about desperately in the water as the friends boarded the navy ship. Lydia immediately headed up to the wheel and had her friends quickly unfurl the sails, but the guards on one of the other jetties had spotted them and had begun to fire their weapons in warning.

'They're blowing holes through the sails!' yelled Lydia. 'We need to retaliate, quick, arm the cannons! Make sure you don't kill those guards though!'

Vincent and Mel rapidly armed the cannons and fired, destroying part of the jetty and forcing the guards to retreat. At that moment, Lydia turned the ship towards Cyril's path and they sailed away.

'Vincent?' she said.

Vincent turned to her.

'Do you think you could fix those holes in the sails?'

'I don't see how,' said Vincent. 'But I'll go below deck and see what I can find.'

'Please be quick,' said Lydia. 'We've been delayed enough as it is.'

Cyril and the centaurs were a short distance beyond Acrodryohydrus Island, sailing through warm, tropical water which was not quite clear. Their ship was just visible to some of the children who were being kept safely on the island.

'If you're finding it too hot out here, you can find shelter indoors,' said Cyril. 'But make sure you stay close, so you can hear me if I call for you.'

Suddenly, one of the centaurs noticed some strange waves and ripples in the water and caught sight of what looked like some scaly skin. He called the Prince over.

'Your Highness? You should come and see this.'

Cyril came down onto the lower deck and looked over the side, to discover what appeared to be at least two sea monsters circling in the water. He couldn't quite tell what they were, but Cyril was taking no chances.

'We'll have to sail the ship out into open water, away from the island,' said Cyril. 'We don't want to cause the children any panic.'

They sailed for a few minutes with the sea monsters following close behind, before dropping anchor at a safe distance.

'Men, arrows at the ready,' said Cyril. 'Take aim at those creatures in the water down there. Ready? Fire!'

The centaurs fired their arrows, most of which plunged into the monsters' skin. The creatures thrashed about in pain and immediately disappeared, diving deep beneath the ship.

'I'll just go down to the viewing glass and see if those

animals are close enough for me to identify them,' said Cyril.

He ran down to the observation chamber in the ship's hull and looked out of the glass, searching for the monsters. One silhouette moved closer to the ship and into the light, and Cyril could see that it was just an ordinary sea dragon, with arrows sticking out of its scaly skin. They'd attacked the wrong animals.

'Confounded creatures!' he said to himself. 'Lawrence, what I'd do for your help right now…'

Lydia was several miles behind, east of Cyril's position in shallower water. The holes in the sails had been sewn over with serviettes from the galley, and Lydia and Lawrence were both behind the wheel.

'The water's very clear now,' said Lydia. 'We can just about see the creatures below. Is it clear enough for you to recognise them, Lawrence?'

'I can certainly give it a go, the larger ones should be easy enough to identify at least,' said Lawrence. 'Steer the ship carefully, will you?'

The witches, meanwhile, were sitting on the deck with a fishing net as if preparing to catch a large animal, their eyes fixed on the surface as a dark shape moved through the water towards them.

'This one has too many spikes,' said the tailed witch. 'Leave it.'

'No, it could be a new species,' said the pink-eyed witch.

'Roll up the sails,' ordered Lydia. 'What's going on

down there?'

She headed down to the side of the ship and spotted one of the dragons that Cyril had attacked earlier. It swam underneath the ship and in the opposite direction to which Lydia was facing, allowing Lydia to see the centaur's arrows in its sides.

'Did you see what I saw?' she asked Lawrence, as she came back up to the wheel.

'It looked like a sea dragon, turned into a pin-cushion by arrows,' said Lawrence, sadly. 'And those arrows, if I'm not mistaken, are centaur arrows. Cyril is near, Lydia.'

They both gazed into the distance ahead, lost in thought for a moment, before Lydia caught sight of movement on the horizon. She grabbed Lawrence's arm and pointed. More sea dragons. Unlike the dragon they had seen a moment ago, these sea dragons had bright blue skin, large eyes and curvaceous bodies, and were all travelling close together.

As they drew nearer, Lawrence made his way to the lower deck to help Vincent and Mel quietly prepare the cannons, leaving Lydia at the helm. The dragons soon reached the front of the ship and emerged from the water, holding themselves upright, and they proceeded to stare directly at Lydia.

'Is a certain prince aboard this vessel?' asked one dragon.

'No, but we're searching for him, too,' said Lydia.

The dragon closest to the ship rested the front of its body on the side, looking Lydia in the eye and rocking the ship slightly. 'I will find him before you do. He is ours to hunt down and bring back to the pages of time. He needs to learn a lesson.'

'Vincent! Mel! Now!' yelled Lydia.

Two cannons were fired, striking the water next to the dragons and scaring them into a descent. One of them came back up again near the back of the ship, where E.V. was standing. E.V. opened her wooden case, took out what looked like a handkerchief and threw it onto the dragon's nose. It took a moment, but the dragon became sleepy and crashed down flat on the water, remaining motionless. Meanwhile, Vincent and Mel kept firing the cannons into the water, until all the dragons retreated.

'Are they gone?' Lydia asked Lawrence.

'It's difficult to tell, they are blue after all,' said Lawrence.

'E.V., what did you throw at that dragon just now?' asked Lydia.

'A touch of chloroform,' said E.V. 'A touch in this case being an entire handkerchief dipped in a bottle of liquid. As far as I'm aware, I've just drowned the animal.'

Suddenly, arrows came flying up from the other side of the ship.

'What's that?' exclaimed Lydia.

'Something tells me those aren't centaur arrows,' said Lawrence.

Lydia looked over the other side and saw a school of mer-people bobbing in the water. Unlike the mer-people in Lawrence's book, these beings had colourful, sparkly fish tails, smooth human torsos and cartoonish human facial features. However, despite their gaudy, immature appearance, they were all holding bows and arrows, so Lydia could not dismiss them entirely.

'Don't tell me, you're looking for Prince Cyril?' sighed Lydia.

'That's right,' said the mer-people.

'Since those dragons were too big to search your ship...' said one of them.

'We'll come aboard and search it instead,' finished another.

Lydia immediately aimed her pistol at the group of mer-people and fired a shot into the water beside them. 'Be gone, you savages!'

But the mer-people simply fired more arrows, which Lydia narrowly dodged.

'Shall we have Vincent and Mel draw these ones off too?' asked Lawrence.

'You go down and tell them,' said Lydia. 'I'm going to continue this mission. Unfurl the sails!' she cried as Lawrence hurried inside.

The witches and E.V. quickly unfurled the sails and Lydia steered the ship right over the mer-people, forcing them to swim away. After a few moments of ploughing through the water, all was calm and quiet again.

'Who wants a bite to eat, then?' asked Lydia cheerily.

Whilst Lydia and the others were busy preparing their meal, Cyril was patrolling the warm water, on the lookout for more immature creatures.

'I'm hungry,' he grumbled to one of the centaurs nearby. 'Are you hungry as well?'

'A little, Your Highness,' admitted the centaur. 'At this rate, we may have to fish for our food.'

'I understand now that fishing is traditional for most predators,' said Cyril. 'There may be some salt and pepper in the galley. I know that there are plates and dishes. We just need a net…'

But then they saw the immature mer-people approaching them from the front.

'We'll worry about food in a few minutes,' decided Cyril. 'Take up attack positions!'

The centaurs rolled up the sails and prepared as many arrows as they could. The battle of the arrows was intense and deadly and Cyril decided to go inside for cover. But before he could do so, he was struck in the shoulder by an arrow and cried out in pain. Some of the centaurs were struck too, and one of them, having heard Cyril's cry, grabbed him and ushered him inside. Cyril, with the arrow still stuck in his shoulder, turned his face back to the deck.

'Man the cannons and fire at will!' he ordered, before the doors closed behind him.

The centaurs immediately went down to the lower deck, armed the cannons and managed to fire them. Cyril heard the booming from inside.

'I feel so helpless with a battle going on out there,' he said to the centaur.

'I understand, Your Highness,' said the centaur. 'But there's little you can do whilst injured. Now, this may hurt a little, but I'll do it quickly.'

With lightning speed, the centaur pulled the arrow out of Cyril's shoulder, almost making him scream.

'Oh, that feels better,' gasped Cyril.

The battle outside was still raging.

'I'm sorry you have to be here,' said Cyril. 'A situation like this on land is one thing, but when it happens in the middle of open water, there's not much one can do about it, is there?'

'Don't you worry, Sir,' said the centaur. 'You summoned just the right animals for this quest. We're born to be heroic. If we must die in order to save you, we, like those soldiers of yours, are willing to make that sacrifice.'

Cyril rested his hand on the centaur's shoulder in gratitude.

By the time the cannons had stopped firing, some of the mer-people were drifting in the water, dead, along with some of the centaurs, who lay unmoving on the deck. Cyril and the centaur who had saved him, having heard the cease in cannon fire, slowly peeked outside, bowing their heads at the devastating scene before them.

'Please, don't prepare the ship to sail again just yet,' said Cyril, sadly. 'Let us all take a moment to mourn.'

Aboard the hijacked navy ship, the witches had prepared lunch in the galley and everyone else, including Lydia, was sitting at the dining table.

'How much longer are you planning to continue this search?' asked Vincent.

'Another hour and then we'll head back,' said Lydia.

She turned around and looked between the red drapes, out of the window.

'I know he's still out there,' she murmured, before standing up and addressing the table. 'I must just go and check on the witches.'

She left the dining room and headed into the galley, where the witches were cooking with two cauldrons.

'How is it going?' she asked.

'We've got a separate cauldron for the vegetarians this time,' said the tailed witch. 'We've just started making the soup.'

The pink-eyed witch came over to the cauldron with some greenery.

'You won't need to put those beanstalk leaves into the soup,' said Lydia. 'And don't chop the potatoes. What are those eggs for?'

'Just to add flavour,' said the pointy-eared witch. 'I've added some already.'

'What?' said Lydia. 'You can't serve people eggs on a ship!'

'Why not?'

'Because it's sickly food. It's more likely to make us seasick when we move again. On the other hand, if you've added some already, I suppose a few more won't make a difference. Just don't tell anyone else.'

The centaurs aboard the Royal Sailing Ship were dumping the bodies of the dead centaurs overboard, as the ship made its way back towards the mainland. Cyril was lying down in one of the cabins, exhausted.

The centaur who had saved him was keeping him company. 'It is a pity we didn't bring a proper doctor with us, Your Highness.'

'Or a cook,' remarked Cyril. 'I'm still hungry. I've never felt so weak.'

Another centaur came into the room. 'Your Highness? There's something large in the distance. It could be a fellow sailing ship.'

Cyril stood up and made his way slowly to the main deck. He could see another ship approaching them and could hear somebody calling his name, but he couldn't quite make out who it was. As the ship drew closer, Cyril recognised the cry and headed to the front of his ship.

'Lydia?' he yelled.

'Cyril!' cried Lydia.

'I don't believe it!' said Cyril. 'Come on, everyone. Let's get some rope and connect these ships.'

'Quick, see if you can find some rope,' said Lydia to her group.

After a moment of searching, both crews threw ropes over to the other ship and held on until the ships' port sides were parallel with each other. Then, with all their might, they pulled the two ships together. Cyril and Lydia reached across and hugged each other.

'I can't understand how you manage to keep finding me,' said Cyril.

To his surprise, Finnegan came up onto the deck of Lydia's ship.

'I don't believe *this* either.'

'Are you alright, Cyril?' asked Finnegan.

'Yes, apart from a bad shoulder.' Cyril displayed the hole in his coat.

'Oh, did you get hit by an arrow then?' said Lydia. 'I am sure E.V. could see to that.'

But just then, the ships rocked violently, as though something had crashed into them, and everyone knew they were in danger again. Cyril went to the starboard side of his ship and saw the school of mer-people down below in the water. Meanwhile, Lydia went to the starboard side of *her* ship and spied the faces of the sea dragons in the water. They both ran back to where the two ships connected.

'I feel a little more confident with you here to help me, Lydia,' said Cyril. 'Okay, centaurs, arrows at the ready!'

'Man the cannons!' ordered Lydia.

The two groups prepared their weapons before Cyril and Lydia screamed, 'Fire!'

The centaurs launched their arrows towards the mer-people, while Vincent and Mel fired the cannons on Lydia's ship at the dragons. Cyril noticed that some of the centaurs on his ship were preparing the cannons.

'I've got an idea,' he said to Lydia, as they came to the middle again.

They got the attention of their crews and waved them

over.

'Now!' said Cyril.

Quickly, the groups switched ships, and therefore attackers, confusing the enemy such that when the arrows and cannons were fired again, the mer-people and sea dragons began to panic, fearful of the sudden change in weaponry. It seemed to frighten them off, but not for long. They made U-turns in the water and swam straight back for more. As the battle progressed, Lydia had an idea of her own, which she immediately went to tell Cyril.

'Isn't that dangerous?' asked Cyril.

'Of course,' said Lydia. 'Otherwise, it wouldn't be worth a try.'

Without hesitation, they each went down into the hull of their own ships to collect a couple of barrels of gunpowder, arriving back on deck within minutes. Lydia threw her two barrels over the free side of her ship and aimed her pistol at them, while Cyril threw his over the free side of the Royal Sailing Ship and asked one of the centaurs to set an arrow alight.

'Ready? Aim…' commanded Cyril.

Lydia and the centaur aimed at the floating barrels.

'Fire!' ordered Cyril.

The two of them fired, striking their targets with upmost precision. The water on either side of the ships erupted, as the gunpowder was set alight and transformed into a mass of flame and smoke. It certainly frightened off the dragons and the mer-people this time, causing great waves as the force of the blasts shifted the water. The ropes holding the two ships together nearly snapped, but just about held firm as the water slowly calmed down again. There was a long silence.

'I think we did it,' said Lydia.

'Yes, we did!' exclaimed Cyril.

Once more, the two groups gave a huge cheer, and also threw up their hats, relieved to have ended the day victorious.

A little while later, Cyril was sitting on one of the outside staircases of the Royal Sailing Ship, contemplating the events of the day.

Lydia spotted him and walked over to the edge of her ship's deck, so they could talk. 'So…' she said. 'When do we go back?'

'Well, now that you mention it, my stomach would certainly like to go back,' said Cyril. 'I haven't even had any lunch today.'

'So, you're not only wounded, but ravenous as well,' sighed Lydia. 'The witches can make you some dinner now, if you like.'

'A few raw vegetables would do. I'm not in the mood for anything much. Lydia, I've been meaning to ask…did the navy let you borrow that ship?'

'Well, not exactly…I may have been a little persuasive.'

'Don't think, just because of another success, that I shan't send you to the authorities for an offense like this,' said Cyril sternly.

Lydia raised her eyebrows at him.

'*I'm* the one those animals want,' continued Cyril. 'And by getting involved, you've doubled the commotion and made us more vulnerable to these immature beasts.'

'Cyril…' said Lydia, somewhat exasperated. 'I did this with the best intentions. I wanted to protect you, since you seem fairly incapable of protecting yourself. But if punishing me will make you stop going out on these ridiculous quests, then I will willingly go to the authorities. Go ahead, arrest me why don't you?'

'You…you mean you actually *want* me to?' said Cyril.

'Well, unless you'd rather have teenagers risk their lives for you,' said Lydia bitterly.

'What are you talking about?'

'Don't you know why the navy was out training today? Another enlistment of teenaged males has been requested to join, to protect you. They were out doing exercises.'

'What?' exclaimed Cyril. 'I thought we'd sent all children to Acrodryohydrus Island.'

'Maybe you didn't realise who 'children' would include on this occasion,' said Lydia. 'Apparently they need all the young males from post-school onward in training. Now, some are perfectly willing, but they don't all want to fight, they're children! You won't believe the things some of them are doing to try and get out of it. Many of the older girls have sworn to go into battle; they don't see why their younger brothers should have to fight when they don't. If we don't risk our lives for you, they will. So, if you want to have me punished…'

'No, wait,' said Cyril. 'I can't let those children…*my* children, risk their lives for me.'

'You're no father yet, Cyril,' said Lydia. 'But you already have the compassion of one. These challenging

212

times are poisoning the compassion in our Kingdom; it is fortunate that you're still willing to show it, now and again.'

'I will request an explanation from those parents of mine,' said Cyril. 'They have yet again set a poor example for me to follow. I shall pardon you Lydia, for now. Fetch me a bite to eat, would you? Then we'll turn these ships around.'

Within the next hour, Cyril and Lydia arrived back at the dock with the two ships. The sun was beginning to set, elongating their shadows on the decks.

'What are you planning to do next, Cyril?' asked Lydia.

'We've only scared the immature animals away,' said Cyril. 'They will be back if we don't go down there...'

'Where?'

'To the pages of time. I need to teach them a lesson.'

'But you have no idea what might happen to you down there,' said Lydia. 'You might not succeed or even return.'

'Too much is being based on a 'might',' said Cyril. 'I need to go and do it for real, like I have been over the last few weeks. Besides, who *wants* to return if they don't succeed?'

'Try not to sound too much like your ancestors, Your Highness,' said Lydia. 'Though I suppose it's only fair in the present situation for at least one member of the royal family to be involved.'

She gave Cyril a hug and left without another word.

Cyril turned to the surviving centaurs. 'I am truly sorry for the loss of your friends and I'm immensely grateful for your dedication to my cause. This is where we part, for you cannot come with me to where I am going next. All that remains is for me to say thank you.'

The King and Queen were taking a stroll around the outside of their tree, just as the toadstools were starting to light up.

'I feel certain something's happened to him this time,' worried the Queen. 'I refuse to eat until they come back.'

'My dear, if I know Cyril, he's a survivor,' said the King. 'He's always been determined, and he hasn't given up on his cause ever since what happened at the opera house.'

'I'm going to go and find him,' said the Queen, impatiently.

But it was at that moment that Cyril and Finnegan appeared at the gates. Cyril was on foot.

The Queen immediately ran over to them. 'Cyril! Finnegan! You're…alive!'

'Yes, we are,' said Cyril wearily.

The guards rapidly unlocked the gates, and once they were inside, Cyril ran straight into his mother's arms.

'Are you hurt?' asked the Queen.

'Not much, just an arrow to the shoulder,' said Cyril, drawing their attention to the hole in his coat created by the arrow. 'But I'm okay, and so is Finnegan.'

The Queen took a deep breath through her nose, and a strange scent caught her attention. 'Is that brandy I smell?'

'Yes, I found some aboard the ship, or on one of the ships,' said Cyril. 'It's almost like medicine. It made me feel a lot better after that battle.'

'I'm not surprised,' remarked the King.

'Would you like me to take a look at that injury?' asked the Queen, ignoring the King's amused expression.

'E.V.'s already sorted it,' said Cyril. 'She's a good doctor, I'm glad I gave her a second chance.'

'Are you done with fighting animals then, Cyril?' asked the King.

'I've barely started…' said Cyril.

CHAPTER X

A BLOSSOMING BRANCH

Prince Cyril was nearing full maturity, and though his parents, along with his friends Lydia and Lawrence, had done their best to guide him, Cyril had made the mistake of thinking he could change nature. This had led to a disaster for which he was determined to make up to his parents. He had found himself in danger several times recently. Now, he wanted to go underneath the map, to the pages of time, to personally confront the immature creatures that had tried to take over their world. After his last escapade, Cyril hadn't spoken a lot, spending much of his time wandering the grounds and staring off into space. It had been a peaceful time, but he had left his parents feeling more worried than ever.

Early one morning, Cyril awoke in the darkness, dressed himself and crept down the quiet staircase to the stable, ready to tackle his most epic task yet. The horses were all asleep when he arrived.

'Psst, Finnegan,' whispered Cyril.

Finnegan did not respond, so Cyril entered his pen and shook him a little. Eventually, the horse woke up.

'Cyril?'

'Sshh, everyone else is still sleeping,' whispered Cyril. 'The time has come, Finnegan. I'm going to those pages today.'

Finnegan looked out beyond the stable doors at the silhouette of the distant hills. 'Can I have some breakfast first?'

'You can have breakfast at the Flying-Horse-for-Hire stable,' said Cyril. 'That's where we're going.'

'Your parents will kill me for this,' grumbled Finnegan. 'I always give them my word to protect you. On the other hand, that doesn't mean I can't take you to a harmless stable I suppose…' Finnegan sighed. 'If it is your wish, I shall take you. You do know that whoever guards that stable sleeps inside at night.'

'No, I didn't know that,' said Cyril. 'That will make things tougher…ah well, just leave it to me. I'll work something out. Now, come on, and be quiet.'

They sneaked out of the stable and down to the gates, where the guards were standing, straight and tall as ever. They spoke for a while, but eventually Cyril managed to convince the guards to concede to his request and the gates were opened.

Finnegan and Cyril journeyed through the forest brimming with the early morning chorus of birdsong, but as they emerged from the trees beside the flying horse stable, the two friends fell silent.

'The doors are closed,' murmured Cyril. 'The animals must be inside. This is going to be tricky.'

In the stable, the little owner was sleeping on a mattress, placed snugly inside a wooden box which had then been hung on the wall like a shelf. There were small, ladder-like steps connected to the wall beside it.

A knock at the door woke the sleeping owner and he climbed down his little ladder to answer it. Finnegan was waiting outside.

'Good morning,' said the owner sleepily.

'I'm sorry to disturb you,' said Finnegan. 'I'm the young Prince's horse.'

'I remember you,' said the owner, as the flying horses started to wake up. 'You'd better come in.'

'No, no...' said Finnegan. He went on talking as the doors at the back of the stable quietly began to open. 'The Prince has escaped; I came to ask whether you would help me look for him? If we both wait outside, we will be able to spot him if he appears.'

'Be careful what you say, Finnegan,' whispered Cyril to himself, from the other side of the back doors.

He opened the doors a little wider so the flying horses could see him. Gomez, whom Cyril had ridden before, immediately recognised the young Prince and stepped forward, bowing his head.

'I presume your illness has healed now, Your Highness?'

'Yes, I hope you're okay too, Gomez. Listen, there isn't much time.'

Finnegan had turned the owner's attention to the sea, when suddenly, they saw a flyer appear in the sky.

'Gomez!' yelled the owner.

Gomez didn't say anything. The owner went back into the stable to find the back doors open.

He looked at Finnegan again. 'I *knew* there was something suspicious going on.'

Back at Cyril's home, the King and Queen were out of bed but still in their sleepwear. One of the guards was with them in their bedroom, explaining what Cyril had done.

'You fool!' exclaimed the Queen, reaching for the guard's badge.

'I wouldn't do that…' said the King, quickly. 'We'll need all the support we can get if we're to take action this time.'

The Queen turned to the King and began to weep into his chest. 'How could they let Cyril do this?'

'Please, Ma'am,' said the guard. 'You may call me a fool again, but I did not think he was actually serious about what he said he was doing. Shall we go and find him?'

'Yes,' said the King firmly. 'We'll need to send a pigeon

to two of our friends for help first, but once they have been sent for, we will go and find him.'

'Cyril wanted to do this alone,' said the Queen. 'But he'll still need every skill to succeed and I'm not sure he'll accomplish it. Tell half of the soldiers to stand by, excluding those in adolescence. Meanwhile, I must send those letters to our friends, and a third one to Prince Matthias. We will leave in half an hour.'

While the guard sent a carrier pigeon to the Army Base, the Queen sent one to Lydia.

Lydia was in her bedroom when the Queen's pigeon landed on her window ledge, and once she had read the letter, she sent out some pigeons of her own.

The weather was growing colder and windier as Cyril and Gomez flew through the dim southern sky towards the ice caps. Despite the lack of light, they could just about see the land below and eventually reached the huge, icy waterfall.

'Land here,' said Cyril.

Gomez lowered his legs and landed on an iceberg, right next to the avalanche of water.

Cyril set foot on the ice and stepped right onto the edge, observing the clouds below. 'We have to go down there. That's where all these immature animals are coming from: the pages of time.'

'I can't go down there, Your Highness,' said Gomez anxiously.

'You won't exactly need to,' said Cyril. 'Just fly me

down gently, drop me on the ground whilst hovering and then fly back up here.'

'But how will you get back?'

'I'll think of something. I'm always encouraged when I'm past the point of no return.'

Wings trembling from the cold, Gomez allowed Cyril to climb onto his back again and they soared down through the clouds…

Whilst Cyril urged Gomez down beyond the clouds, the King and Queen were in the stable back at their home, preparing to leave. They were both dressed in protective trousers, boots and coats, and the Queen had left her hair untied.

'Are you sure about this?' asked the King. 'Can you be courageous and ride at high speed?'

'We won't come back without our child,' said the Queen. 'If this doesn't persuade him to grow up, nothing will. After all, he's convinced that actions speak louder than words.'

They held each other close and shared a brief but tender kiss, before bringing their horses, Trevor and Gillian, out of their pens.

'We may not need you for long,' the Queen informed them.

'To go off the edge of the map, Cyril will have had to fly across the sea,' explained the King.

The horses nodded sombrely and allowed the King and Queen, clutching their swords, to lead them out of the stable into the early morning sunlight.

By now, Cyril and Gomez were nearing the ground on the page below the map and as they drew closer, Cyril became increasingly aware that both he and Gomez were undergoing some sort of transformation. Instead of their usual selves, they appeared to be in a new dimension or form, as if they had been drawn by a child, all rough shapes and scribbled colours. As they emerged from the clouds, they came across a colourful, hilly landscape, covered in flowers and toadstools.

'I feel quite odd,' said Cyril.

'As do I, Your Highness,' said Gomez nervously.

'Hover here for a moment,' said Cyril. 'This looks like a good place for you to drop me.'

Gomez looked uncertain but allowed Cyril to jump off his back and land on the vibrant, green grass.

'You can go back, Gomez,' said Cyril. 'Go on, go now.'

'Stay out of trouble, Your Highness,' warned Gomez, as he flew up and away.

At the gateway to the city, between the two towers of the great wall, Lydia had assembled her team – Lawrence, E.V., the witches, Mel and Vincent – and they were all standing patiently, waiting for the King and Queen to arrive. Lydia was chewing anxiously on a handful of grass, trying desperately to sooth her nerves.

'You don't need to worry, Lydia,' said Vincent, gently patting her shoulder. 'We're all here to help you find him.'

'He's the Prince, though,' said Lydia. 'He's their son. This is possibly the biggest favour the King and Queen will ever ask; I can't let them down!'

'We're here to help too, you know,' said a voice from behind.

They turned to see Prince Matthias astride his horse, Caroline, alongside an army of his soldiers. The soldiers were all on foot and were equipped with rifles and swords.

'You're Lydia, aren't you?' said Matthias, climbing down from Caroline.

'I am.' Lydia shook his hand. 'Are you one of Cyril's relatives?'

'I'm his uncle, Matthias.'

'I see you've brought quite an army with you,' said Lydia.

'Oh, these are just some of the men from the headquarters in the city,' said Matthias. 'The King and Queen should be arriving any minute now with more of them.'

A few minutes later, the King and Queen arrived as promised, riding on their horses ahead of a platoon of soldiers.

'Matthias!' exclaimed the King.

'Hello, big brother,' said Matthias. 'We don't have many men, do we?'

'That's because there's only a small number of flying horses,' explained the Queen. 'Some of us will have to share. We've assigned every flyer from the stable, but some of our relatives are bringing their own for support. That must be them now.'

She pointed out a whole herd of flying horses in the sky above. Cyril's cousins, Mary and Fergus, were leading them and they gracefully landed on the nearby stretch of grass.

'Mary! Fergus!' said the King. 'I'm glad to see you're here at last. I hope it wasn't too much trouble organising these flying servants.'

'Well, that's why it's good to have at least two people who know how to handle them,' said Fergus.

'Mary?' asked Matthias.

'Yes, Papa?' Mary replied.

'How familiar are they with cold weather?'

'Hopefully enough to stay airborne.'

'Your attention, everyone,' announced the Queen, as she climbed off Gillian. 'We will need to go to the Flying-Horse-for-Hire stable to supply ourselves with more transportation. Mary and Fergus will take the herd back into the sky and we will follow from the ground. Miss Lydia and Mr Toadstool, I must have a word with you. The rest of you can make a head start. We'll catch up. Let us go forth and rescue the heir to our Kingdom's throne!'

Everyone else raced off towards the coast, led by Prince Matthias, while the King and Queen remained behind to speak to Lawrence and Lydia.

'I want both of you to know that you have each played a vital role in changing the Prince's behaviour over the past year,' said the Queen. 'His father and I are truly grateful to you for your support, and in return, we wish to make you an offer. Mr Lawrence Toadstool, I know that you almost lost our respect during one occasion, but you came back hoping to make up for it, and for that we commend you. The Prince might never have understood the difference between imagination and reality without your guidance. Therefore, if this task is a success, we shall honour you with a knighthood.'

'Thank you, Your Majesty,' said Lawrence.

The Queen squeezed his hands, smiling warmly, and hugged him, before turning to Lydia.

'Miss Lydia Hugo, your guidance, and your dedication to the protection of our son, has also been most valuable and we wish to honour that. If we succeed today, I have two options for you: you may henceforth introduce yourself as Dame Lydia, or alternatively as The Duchess of Hugo if you are willing to give our son the privilege of your hand in marriage.'

There was a long pause as Lydia considered the Queen's offer. Yes, Cyril drove her crazy sometimes, and there was still much he needed to learn…but despite all that, Lydia loved him and she knew for certain that he loved her. What was married life without a few challenges along the way? Her mind made up, she turned to face the Queen, her blushing rose pink crests revealing her choice.

'I accept your offer and opt for marriage, Your Majesty,' she said, smiling warmly. 'Thank you, Ma'am.'

'Please, you may as well call me 'Mum' now,' said the Queen brightly. 'Cyril always had so much trouble trying to tell those two forms of address apart. He was relieved when he finally realised that his family did not include half the Kingdom!'

They both gave a chuckle and hugged each other.

'I suppose we are all technically family though, aren't we?' said Lydia.

'Yes, I suppose we are,' said the Queen.

'Right,' said the King. 'Shall we get a move on, then?'

The Queen nodded, climbing onto Gillian and all of them set off towards the coast, Lawrence and Lydia on foot.

In his immature-drawing form, on the lower page, Cyril was pacing through a forest by a stream.

'I know you're here somewhere!' he cried out, to any creature that might be able to hear him. 'Come out and fight!'

He stood still for a moment, trying to decide which way to go next, when a tribe of red-skinned, pointy-eared humanoids appeared from behind the trees in front of him, armed with bows and arrows. One particularly intimidating individual stepped in front of Cyril. He had a heavy build, downward-facing eyebrows and decorations all over his body.

'So, you are Prince Cyril, are you?' he said.

'Yes, that's me,' said Cyril. 'Thought you could frighten *me*, did you?'

'We are the Evil Elves of Immaturity,' said the humanoid. 'I understand you caused a disturbance on the upper page. Were you attempting to forget about us?'

'No, I don't want to forget you…' said Cyril, drawing his sword and holding it towards the elf with both hands. 'I want to destroy you!'

The elf immediately pulled out a sword of his own and he and Cyril clashed weapons. They were both equally skilled, parrying against each other for a long while, until the elf signalled imperceptibly to his tribe. The next time the elf and Cyril broke apart, one of the other elves fired an arrow that plunged into the ground at Cyril's feet. Cyril looked down and jumped back, but it was merely a distraction, allowing two more elves to grab Cyril by the arms and disable his sword.

'This one is a stubborn young thing,' said the lead elf. 'Let's keep him with us, he could be quite valuable. You two, bind him. We shall take him to the fortress.'

The King, Queen and their army were journeying over the sea on the flying horses. For the first time in a long time, wind rushed through the Queen's hair and despite her son's imminent peril, she could not help but enjoy the sensation.

'It's getting colder,' said Lawrence. 'It shouldn't be long now before we reach the ice caps.'

As the flying army approached the edge of the map, Gomez, who was pacing around one of the nearby forest islands, saw the commotion in the sky and immediately flew up to see what was going on.

'Right, hover here,' instructed Lawrence, as the army came to just beyond the waterfall. 'We'll have to go down one at a time,' continued Lawrence. 'I think it would be fair for me to go first.'

Just then, Gomez appeared, hovering with them unseen for a moment until the Queen noticed him.

'There's an unmanned horse here,' exclaimed the Queen. 'Oh, goodness, nobody has fallen, have they?'

Gomez immediately flew towards the Queen and

bowed his head. 'Your Majesty?'

'Yes?' the Queen replied.

'My name is Gomez. I'm the horse who took your royal son to that page down there. I've felt guilty ever since and have been lingering on an island not far from here, contemplating returning to the page below to try and find him. If you are attempting to rescue him, the least I can do is help.'

'Well, that's very thoughtful, Gomez,' said the Queen. 'You won't have to answer to your owners. I'll explain everything to them for you. For now, do you think you could guide us down there?'

'Certainly, Madam,' said Gomez.

'Lawrence here was just about to take the plunge,' said the King. 'You can show him down there first.'

Gomez escorted Lawrence and his flying horse down through the clouds and everyone gradually followed, one behind the other.

The elves were approaching their red and black fortress, complete with flags, battlements and jail bars, and Cyril looked terrified, even though the fortress looked like a drawing and not like a real fortress at all.

'You'll never get away with this, you savages!' he yelled. 'My parents will come to save me, you'll see!'

'Is that right?' said the lead elf. 'And how are they going to get past all those obstacles back there?'

'They'll get past a few babyish dragons and some immature water creatures easily,' said Cyril fiercely. 'They love me, and they won't give up on me.'

'You think love is as powerful as you say, do you?' said the elf. 'You will see soon enough.'

They dragged Cyril into the fortress, up a flight of stairs, and threw him into a jail cell. It was cold, hard and dark, with the exception of the flickering strips of light that shone through the bars onto the floor.

'How long are you going to keep me here?' asked Cyril.

'You are the bait in our trap, Your Highness,' stated the elf. 'We shall keep you here long enough to give your companions time to reach this fortress, and then, when they're exhausted from fighting, we will complete our mission and overthrow the world!'

He and the other elves cackled and walked away, leaving Cyril alone to contemplate his fate.

The King, Queen and their army had landed on the lower page, and they were all staring at one another's changed appearances. Just as Cyril and Gomez had experienced, the entire company had transformed into childlike drawings. Many of the women had larger hips and longer eyelashes and their long hair had been tied up in pigtails, whilst many of the men had broader shoulders and more pronounced facial features, and all the soldiers suddenly had red coats with white sashes, tall hats and bushy moustaches. They could still more or less identify one another by their faces.

'Is…is that you?' they all started asking each other in confusion.

Gomez, having already been through this change, quickly explained to the company what was happening, and they all breathed a huge sigh of relief.

The Queen looked around. 'Where shall we start then?'

'Well, you see those animals over there?' said Lawrence. 'If Cyril's plan was to confront them, then that's where he must have gone.'

'Right, you can climb off your horses, people,' instructed the Queen. 'We are not flying; we are going down that hill on foot, towards the forest. There may be clues as to where Cyril has been, and we must also do what he set out to do: destroy these monsters!'

Once they had reached the bottom of the hill and were nearing the trees, Vincent and Mel stopped to gaze at some of the scenery.

'This brings back many memories.' Mel was looking at two big stones or boulders that had been engraved with some kind of lettering.

'I'd truly forgotten,' murmured Vincent.

He had his eyes on the artistic landscape, with its fluffy clouds and gaudy rainbow.

'We must spend a moment or two here,' said Mel.

'Yes, our minds are so transfixed,' said Vincent. 'These are the kinds of things that inspired our abilities and talents.'

The King, noticing that Vincent and Mel were lagging behind, sighed and turned to a couple of the soldiers. 'Fetch those children, would you?'

The soldiers held their swords by the handle, in case they needed to draw them, and marched over to Vincent and Mel.

'Come on then, lads,' they said.

'All in good time,' said Vincent.

The soldiers looked at each other then took out their swords, holding them in front of Mel and Vincent.

'Sorry to have to do this to you,' said one of them.

'But we have our orders,' said the other.

Slowly, Mel and Vincent turned away from the scenery and dragged themselves in the King's direction, their heads bowed.

'Some people never learn,' sighed the King.

As they were walking alongside a small stream in the depths of the forest, the Queen suddenly stopped. She had found Cyril's sword on the forest floor.

'Is this Cyril's?' she asked her husband.

'If it didn't have such childish detail, I'd say it was,' said the King.

'What a relief!' said the Queen. 'We are finally getting somewhere. Lawrence, here, take Cyril's sword. You should have a weapon of your own, especially since you have such a detailed understanding of these animals; out of all of us, you will know best where to strike.'

She handed Lawrence the sword.

'Thank you, Ma'am,' said Lawrence. 'I was hoping it wouldn't come to this.'

'Hold onto it until we've rescued Cyril,' said the Queen. 'And I shall knight thee with that very sword.'

As the army emerged from the forest, they found themselves in front of their first obstacle. Dragons. These dragons were perched on a rugged, rocky outcrop and had the same bright green scales as the immature dragons that had attacked their own world.

'Have your weapons at the ready,' said the King quietly. 'We're going to sneak up on them, through these rocks. If those dragons try to repel us, shoot them.'

The soldiers took aim with their rifles as they all began to make their way to the other side of the valley. A few moments later, one of the dragons spotted them and swooped over.

'I expect you're the ones who are off to save the Prince,' the creature growled.

'We are doing just that,' said the Queen. 'Don't you dare try to stop us now.'

'That's asking us not to do what we have instructions to do…' growled another dragon, who had just appeared before them. 'The elves knew what they were doing when they kidnapped the Prince.'

'The elves?' enquired the King.

The dragons had clearly had enough of small talk, for instead of answering the King's question, they blew out great jets of fire, causing the flying horses to rear back in panic. The soldiers immediately started shooting, and some of them climbed onto the rocks with their swords and swung their weapons at the dragons. After a brief and bloody battle the dragons, weakened by their wounds, all lay dead on the ground. Some of the soldiers also lay unmoving, and many had been seriously injured by the dragon fire.

'E.V., dear?' asked the Queen, gesturing to the injured

soldiers.

'Yes, Ma'am, I'll get to it right away.'

They all took shelter under the cover of a ledge while E.V saw to the casualties and the witches prepared them all a nourishing meal. The Queen sat down beside Matthias as they ate.

'I do hope we don't encounter any more fire-breathers today, Matthias,' said the Queen. 'Haven't some of your men fought dragons before?'

'Yes, in the Reptile Kingdom,' said Matthias. 'It was all a necessary test of bravery, though I never thought it would end up being practice for fighting less mature dragons.'

'I often wonder whether children are more in control of grownups than we are of them…' mused the Queen.

'I have often wondered the same thing myself,' said Matthias. 'We may make the decisions, but they are usually decisions that our children force us to make, for their own good.'

'I just wish I knew whether Cyril was alright,' sighed the Queen, as she turned to Lawrence, who had taken a seat beside them. 'What were those dragons referring to when they said, 'the elves' had kidnapped Cyril?'

'The Evil Elves of Immaturity,' said Lawrence. 'They are the ones who have been sending out these animals to try and hunt down Cyril.'

'What are the chances they have succeeded?'

'Fifty-fifty I would say. It is entirely possible that they are currently holding him hostage, to lure us into a trap.'

Whilst the Queen and Lawrence were discussing Cyril's

possible whereabouts, Vincent and Mel were talking.

'It's understandable that we shouldn't want to destroy our youth all together,' said Vincent. 'After all, without the lessons we learnt as children, we would not be the adults we are today. I think perhaps it is important not to forget those childhood experiences. Those dragons, for example, would make an ideal subject for my paintings every now and then.'

'Yes, and we should also look back on our language development too, and the words we used as children,' said Mel. 'Perhaps they will provide us with insights which we can then teach our descendants.'

Once they had recovered from the dragon battle, the company set about their journey again, travelling further into the unknown world. The injured soldiers were limping slightly from the pain, but E.V. had worked wonders and they were just about managing to keep up with the rest of the army.

As they went on, Lawrence and E.V. fell behind, just as Vincent and Mel had done earlier. The Queen looked back to see where they had got to, to see Lawrence gazing at a herd of dinosaurs on a distant plain, whilst E.V. had turned her attention to a large, wooden obstacle course.

'This is what started my whole obsession with survival skills,' said E.V.

'I can't believe how much more there is to dinosaurs now,' said Lawrence. 'I remember when this was all I thought there was.'

'That will do now,' said the soldiers behind them, again

holding the handles of their swords. 'Keep up and help the Queen like you promised. She's watching you.'

Grabbing Lawrence and E.V. in an arm-lock, the soldiers walked them back over towards the Queen.

'You're taking a once-in-a-lifetime opportunity away from us!' complained Lawrence.

'*Lawrence*,' said the Queen sternly. 'You want to earn that knighthood, don't you?'

'Oh absolutely, Your Majesty,' said Lawrence.

'Please let me take on that obstacle course, Your Majesty, just once,' pleaded E.V.

'Your work here isn't finished yet, E.V.,' said the Queen. 'Now come, let us be strong and put aside our own desires until we have completed our task.'

A little while later, the company came to a massive lake, with a narrow ledge running right through the middle of it, splitting it in two. It looked suspicious.

'Is there no other way to cross the lake?' asked the Queen.

'We could get back on the horses and fly if we take a run-up on that ledge,' said the King. 'There's little room for them to spread their wings on this side of the lake. Soldiers, you two go first. We'll follow.'

The two soldiers the King had addressed climbed onto their horses and cautiously clip-clopped onto the ledge. As the King, Queen and everyone else followed, they started to gallop and gain speed. The soldiers were about to lift off, when a large, blue, snake-like monster soared through the air in an arch from one half of the lake to the other, just missing them. The movement distracted the horses, causing most of them to crash back down onto the ledge. Unfortunately, one of the horses tumbled into the pool the monster had come from, his rider still on his back. The horse was a strong swimmer and began to try and escape the water, but whinnied in terror as another shape began to move through the water towards them.

'Take my hand!' cried the King, running onto the ledge and reaching down to grab onto the soldier.

The soldier took his hand and his horse started flapping again, as if about to take off. But before the King could pull the soldier clear of the water, an immature sea dragon emerged from the water and faced the army.

'You survived then?' growled the dragon.

'Yes, and we're not afraid of you!' shouted the Queen.

The King suddenly felt a tug on his trouser leg and looked around to see a school of mer-people in the other pool, bows and arrows at the ready.

'Soldiers, take out your rifles, and make these creatures leave us alone,' commanded the King.

The soldiers pointed their weapons straight at the mer-people and after a brief moment of consideration, the mer-people lowered their weapons, encouraging the soldiers to lower theirs. Almost immediately, the mer-people swung around, back into the water, splashing the soldiers with their tails, distracting the army long enough for the mer-people to re-emerge and begin firing their arrows. Some soldiers were struck and fell into the pool below.

'Fire!' cried the King.

The remaining soldiers opened fire at the mer-people and the horses tried to lend a hand by hovering above the water and kicking the mer-people. This tactic managed to scare a few of the mer-people away, but predictably, the sea dragon began to attack them again, dragging one of the horses down into a watery grave. Lydia took out her pistol and also tried to help, firing at the mer-people, her face fixed in a horrified grimace as their blood spattered all over the lake. But it wasn't long before the rest of the creatures had fled.

'Let's climb back onto these flyers and get out of here, quickly!' screamed the Queen.

Everyone tried their best; some had to jump into the water in order to climb onto their horses, but they managed it and within minutes, the army was in the air again. The dragon burst out of the water once more, making one last attempt to bring down a flyer, this time Lydia's. Fortunately, it missed, and Lydia, along with everyone else, headed towards the countryside beyond the vast lake.

Once the shrinking army of people and flying horses had successfully crossed the water, they landed and began walking again, making their way through yet more woodland. They were about to proceed through what appeared to be a small patch of orchard, when the three witches stopped, gazing at a number of picnic tables that stood beneath the apple trees.

'Do you remember how we discovered our talent for cooking?' said the pink-eyed witch.

'When we had apples at a picnic table?' suggested the tailed witch.

'No, when we mixed fish with fruit and it tasted awful,' said the pointy-eared witch.

The Queen, noticing the witches, nodded to several of the soldiers, who came up behind the witches and put their hands on their shoulders.

'Don't get too distracted,' they warned.

But Lydia was also distracted; having climbed to the top of the wooded hill they were standing on, she was standing motionless, gazing out over a small town which lay in the valley below.

'I wonder who lives in that town down there?' she mused, speaking to no one in particular.

Lawrence, seeing her on top of the hill, came up behind her to take a look. 'That's where most of the evil elves live. Is something wrong, Lydia?'

'I dreamed of marrying a prince, and ruling a kingdom once, when I was very young, but…' Lydia walked back down the hill and faced the direction that they were supposed to be travelling in. 'I never imagined achieving that dream would involve all this…'

Cyril was still in the jail cell at the fortress, and having been awake since early that morning he was beginning to feel drowsy. As he lay down on the concrete bench, he heard a heavy flapping sound from outside and immediately jumped up and looked out of the window. He saw his parents, Matthias, Lydia, Lawrence and all his other friends standing at the fortress gate.

'Mum! Dad! You've come! It is you, isn't it?'

'Cyril!' cried the King. 'Are you alright?'

'I'm fine now,' said Cyril.

'Enough!' exclaimed the lead elf, who was standing behind the battlements above the fortress drawbridge.

The soldiers were hovering on their flyers above the ground with their rifles pointed to the fortress, and the elves were armed with cannons.

'I'm glad to see you made it here,' said the elf.

'Of course we made it,' said the Queen. 'We are everything a son deserves in life. Now, let our Prince go!'

'Certainly, Your Majesty,' said the elf. 'Just turn your Kingdom on the upper page over to us and we'll return your son to you.'

'Never!' said the King fiercely.

The elf nodded at his fellow elves, who began firing warning shots from the cannons. The soldiers retaliated and there was a brief cacophony of bullets and cannon balls before some of the soldiers flew around the side of the fortress and up to the top. They landed and the soldiers swiftly finished off the enemy with great swings of their swords, enabling the King and Queen to fly up and perch on the roof. Jumping into the fortress through the two roof windows, they found the keys to Cyril's jail cell, opened the door and embraced their son.

'It's going to be alright, Cyril,' said the Queen.

'We've got to get away from here,' the King reminded her.

They quickly climbed out of the windows again and onto their two flying horses, signalling to the rest of the army. Cyril's friends and the soldiers nodded, urging their flyers up and away into the sky.

Cyril, his family, his friends and the flyers, having escaped the dreadful world beyond the map, were all back on the stretch of grass outside the Flying-Horse-for-Hire stable, relaxing on the grass after their tiring ordeal. To their relief, they had returned to their normal forms as soon as they left the lower page.

'I'm overjoyed that you're safe, sweetheart,' said the Queen, holding her son close to her chest.

'You've made a wonderful family of this team of people, Cyril; we're pleased for you,' said the King.

Cyril stood up. 'I'm still so sorry about the opera house.'

His parents rose to join him.

'Cyril, if you had asked for our forgiveness, we would have given it to you,' said the Queen. 'Opera houses can be rebuilt. But family? Friendship? Those are the things you really need to cling to.'

Cyril thought for a moment. 'I also wanted to be the one person to do this task, but now it turns out that everyone *other than me* completed it.'

'We were fighting in your name, Cyril,' said the King. 'Your Kingdom set out to help you.'

'This is your first taste of leadership,' said the Queen. 'Although victory is rarely without sacrifice; some of our soldiers gave their lives for you.'

'Please tell me none of them were adolescents!' said Cyril.

'I promise you, Cyril, I made sure none of the adolescents were involved,' the Queen assured him. 'You're already sounding like a father, as well as a king. Now, there is one more thing to discuss…'

The Queen waved Lydia over. 'You may tell him, Lydia,' she said, smiling broadly.

But as Lydia was about to speak, Cyril interrupted.

'Firstly, Lydia…' said Cyril. 'Thank you for helping me. You have come to my aid on multiple occasions now and I am truly grateful for your dedication. But tell me, how did a girl as young and delicate as you…how were you strong enough, and indeed vicious enough, to lead a group of warriors into the jaws of death? The contrast terrifies me.'

'Well, Cyril,' said Lydia. 'Remember a long while back, when I asked you whether I should worry about other people's expectations of me, regarding my work at the inn?'

'I went quite blank during that conversation, didn't I?' said Cyril. 'I do vaguely remember…'

'You told me that I should decide what's best for me,' said Lydia. 'I've thought about it ever since. I hope you don't think me weird for going against other's expectations…'

'Not at all, Lydia,' said Cyril. 'You must remember, I've made friends with some of the weirdest animals alive. You are quite conventional in comparison. What was it that you were about to tell me just now?'

'Cyril,' said Lydia. 'You may ask me for my hand in marriage.'

Cyril was speechless for a moment, staring at Lydia, before looking over to his parents for confirmation. The King and Queen nodded. Cyril smiled, looking back at Lydia, drawing her close as he gently placed his hand under her chin and tilted her head upwards, kissing her suddenly on the lips and then embracing her tightly.

'Is that a yes then?' asked Lydia when they eventually broke apart.

'Definitely!' Cyril grinned, pulling her into another tight hug, before releasing her again and turning to his parents, a distressed expression on his face. 'Oh, I've just remembered, the children on Acrodryohydrus Island! We've got to have them brought back.'

'It's alright, Cyril,' said the Queen. 'We've kept up to date with reports. Most of the children have suffered a little sunstroke, but all of them are okay. We'll see that they are returned to their parents as soon as possible. Then, once everything is back in order, we shall have to start planning a wedding.'

'You know, Cyril,' said the King. 'Both you and Lydia will take our place someday, by which time you may even have had a child of your own.'

'Really?' said Cyril.

'If that's what you wish,' said the King.

'But remember,' said the Queen. 'The lower pages of youth and childhood will always be there, never forget that. This story could happen all over again…to your own children.'

'Don't worry, Mum,' said Cyril. 'I could never forget.'

Over the next few days, all the children were returned safely from Acrodryohydrus Island and were taken home to their families.

Meanwhile, Cyril and his friends helped the Kingdom's people to rebuild their lives after the devastation caused by the immature creatures.

Then, in early summer, Cyril and Lydia had a very stylish wedding, and they lived happily ever after.

BV - #0005 - 070622 - C16 - 197/132/14 - PB - 9781803780092 - Matt Lamination